Phil & D
Thea
could co

Nancy Ngele

She Carried Pink Geraniums

A True Story of Life and Love in the Early Twentieth Century

Nancy Ngele

xulon
PRESS

She Carried Pink Geraniums
by Nancy Ngele

Printed in the United States of America

Library of Congress Control Number: 2003092974
ISBN 1-591606-80-2

Unless otherwise indicated, Bible quotations are taken from the King James Version.

Xulon Press
www.XulonPress.com

Xulon Press books are available in bookstores everywhere, and on the Web at www.XulonPress.com.

Chapter 1

Emma's nose was pressed against the kitchen window. She had never seen Pa drive the buggy so fast. He hardly slowed down to turn in at the driveway. What a cloud of dust whirled behind him!Then he was helping their neighbor out of the buggy. Emma watched the midwife, Mrs. Van Brocklin, take off her shawl and bonnet on her way into the house.

The lady went straight to Ma's bedroom. A moment later Pa came in, wiping sweat from his face. "Has Aunt Tip seen your new kitten, Emma?"he asked.

"No, I don't think so."

Pa gave a quick knock on Aunt Tip's door at the house across the road. He opened the door and called, "Yoo-hoo!Anybody home here?"

Aunt Tip came toward them on her knees across the kitchen floor. That was the only way she could "walk." Pa took her hand and said, "how's my big sister today?"

"Oh, I'm just fine, Charlie. Hello, Emma, my, how you're growing!Are you six yet?"

"Not 'till my birthday. I'll be six April 23rd. How many days is that, Pa?"

"Just ten more days, Em," Pa said.

"Then I can go to school next year!" Emma's eyes shone.

"Oh, yes, you'll like that, won't you?" Aunt Tip said. "Alice," she called to the maid, "will you see if the teakettle is hot, please?We'd like a pot of tea and some milk and cookies. Why, Emma, what's that you've got in your arms?"

"My new kitten. He just got his eyes open. I call him Tiger Shepherdson."

Pa laughed and said, "Tip, what do you hear from Silas?Will he be coming home soon?"

"Yes, his last letter said they were about to wind up the logging business for the season. He should be home by the first of May. (Uncle Silas Harwood worked in a logging camp all winter to be able to afford a maid for Aunt Tip.)The boys and I"ll really be happy to have 'im home."

"I'm sure you will," Pa said. "Will the boys be going to Good Friday Service this afternoon down at the church?"

"Frank and Chub and Harry may go. You know Jessie is working in Hart now,so he isn't here. Will you folks be going?"

"I guess we'll have to wait and see," he said, and Emma thought she saw him wink at Aunt Tip. She wondered what he meant by that.

"Will Lena be coming home for the weekend from her school?Where is it she's teaching?"

"The Bean Town School near Walkerville, but she'll be home this weekend. Of course Lester and George are at school 'till noon today seein' it's Good Friday. Vina stayed home today to help her mother and Mrs. Van Brocklin."

"Oh, so Mrs. Van Brocklin's there? I see," and Aunt Tip smiled.

Some time later Pa woke Emma, curled up with Tiger Shep on the braided rug. "Well, Em, let's go home now."

"All right, Pa. "Emma gave Aunt Tip a hug, picked up her kitten, and left with Pa. As they crossed the road, Emma heard a strange sound coming from their house. She looked up and said, "Pa, what's that?"

"Must be a kitten," Pa said."

"No, Pa, that's not a kitten. It's a baby!What baby's at our house?"

"We'll have to go and see, Em." She let go of his hand and ran across the yard and up the front steps.

She followed the sound of crying to Ma's bedroom. There was Mrs. Van Brocklin bathing a tiny baby girl. "Ma, whose baby is this?"

Ma looked tired and pale in the big bed, but she said, "Why, Emma, this is our baby. You have a little baby sister. Are you glad?"

"Oh, yes, Ma!"she said, her eyes shining as she looked at the squirming,noisy, red baby. No one had told her about this wonderful event.

Pa was standing beside her by this time, and his eyes were shining too. He took Ma's hand, smiling. "Are you all right, Bessie?"

"Yes, I'll be all right," she said tiredly.

When Mrs. Van Brocklin had finished dressing the baby, she handed her to Pa. Vina came in from the kitchen with a flat-sided, round, glass bottle, shaped like a flask, with milk in it. Vina said, "Ma, I warmed the milk on the stove and tested it with my elbow to see that it wasn't too warm."

Then she put a cap on the bottle with a long rubber tube attached and a nipple at the end. She took the whole thing to the crying baby in Pa's arms. He put the nipple into the baby's mouth, and she was happy as soon as she caught on to how to use it.

Pa told Emma that she had used a bottle like that when she was a baby, but she couldn't remember. It would be wonderful to have their very own baby in the house! She touched the baby's silky dark hair, so different from her own. She wanted to feed her, but Pa said, "You'll have plenty of chances to hold and feed her later, but not 'till she gets a little bit bigger. All right, Big Sister?"

"All right, Pa," she said.

It seemed like forever before Emma could hold and feed Baby Pearl Grace, but Ma said it was only six weeks. Aunt Tip had suggested the name Daisy for the baby, but Aunt Lucy, one of Ma's sisters, put it in the *HART JOURNAL* that "a baby girl, Pearl Grace," had been born to Charlie and Bessie Shepherdson. Aunt Lucy wanted the baby named after her husband, Mr. Perl Thomas.

Emma sat on the spindle couch and held out her arms.Ma placed Pearl carefully on Emma's lap. Then she brought the bottle to feed her.

Emma was thrilled the first time Pearl smiled at her.Emma looked at Pearl's pretty brown eyes, which were like Ma's eyes, Pa said. Then Emma gently stroked Pearl's silky, dark brown curly hair. Emma wished her hair was like that instead of reddish blond and straight, and she wished her eyes were brown instead of blue.

When school opened in September, the four Shepherdsons set off together. The two boys led the way.Lester was 15 and George 12. Vina had just turned 18, and she was the only one wearing shoes. The others would go barefoot until cold weather. The reason Vina was still attending the Sackrider School at 18 was that she was preparing to take the Michigan State Teachers' Exam. She and Emma followed their brothers down the sandy road.

Grings' house on the left, like their own, was painted white with an upright and a wing.Sackrider School was less than half a mile from home, "kitty corner" across from the yellow-brick Sackrider Church up on the hill.

The Tate children were coming over the hill from the east, Rummers, Carrs, and Hodges from the south, and Newberrys from the west. Emma waved at her second cousin Lucile Hodges. She was glad that Lucile would be in her class. Vina showed Emma the privy for the girls at the back of the school yard, closest to the road. "Be sure to use the right one.The boys use the other one."

The school steps seemed high to Emma. She held the pipe rail with one hand and clutched her lunch pail with the other. Inside the entryway were coat hooks on both sides.

When they opened the door to the school room, the teacher, Miss Wylie Smith, smiled and said, "Hello,Vina, and who's this little girl?"

"Hello, Miss Smith. This is my sister Emma."

"Hello, Emma," the pretty lady said. "You'll be in the chart class. Come, and I'll show you where you'll sit." The seats faced the door, with the smallest ones in front. She showed Emma a seat with a desk attached. "You'll sit here, Emma," she said.

Emma slid into the seat. She liked it. It was just her size with plenty of room for another girl. She hoped it would be Lucile. "But where do I put my lunch pail?" Emma asked.

Bring it over here and put it on the shelf near the water pail." Vina pointed to a shelf at the front.From that shelf to the door there was a blackboard.

When the school bell stopped ringing, all the children were sitting down, and to Emma's delight, Lucile was sitting with her. She was happy, but a little scared, too. She didn't know what to expect.

Chapter 2

When Miss Smith walked to the platform at the front, her long skirts swished against the desks. Her long-sleeved white waist was trimmed with lace and a cameo. Her dark curly hair was formed into a neat bun on top of her head. When she reached her desk and turned around, all the children stood up.

"Good morning, Children."

"Good morning, Teacher," the children said, and they sat down.

Miss Smith led them in singing "America" from the *KNAPSACK SONG BOOK*. After "America" they sang "The Old Oaken Bucket" and "When Johnny Comes Marching Home Again."

When it was time for Emma's class, Miss Smith said, "Will the Chart Class please come up now?" They walked up and sat on a long wooden bench in front of the platform. Frank Miller went first, followed by Emma and Lucile. Then came Earl Trommater, Blanche and Grace Hart, Arthur Sills, Charlie Hull, Nathan Tate, and Inez and Leroy Wolf.

Miss Smith taught this class from a set of charts on an easel instead of books. Emma thought this was fun, and she listened with interest to the older children's classes. Emma was sure she was going to like school.

When the school year had nicely started, the Crusaders came to Sackrider Church. After school each day Emma and many other children went over to the church for a children's meeting. The man standing at the front wore a uniform and played a trumpet or a drum when he wasn't telling Bible stories. His wife wore a uniform, too.She sat pumping the organ with her feet and playing it with her hands. Pa said the Crusaders were like the Salvation Army, but their little girl didn't wear a uniform. She wore pretty dresses and bright hair ribbons in her dark curly hair.

On the third day of the children's meetings, Rev. Johnston invited the children to come forward and pray to receive Christ as their Savior. All the children except Emma went up to the altar to pray. She understood what it was all about, but she didn't think many of the children were sincere. She flipped her blond braids over her shoulders. She was not going to join them.

Ma had said that morning, "Emma, we'll have the Johnstons come for supper tomorrow night, so tell them tonight after the children's meeting.Don't forget."

After what seemed like a long time, the service was dismissed, and the children left the altar, a few of them wiping their eyes. "Hm," Emma observed to herself, "I guess some of them did mean it." She walked up to Mrs. Johnston, "Ma said I should invite you to our house for supper tomorrow night."

"Why, that's so nice of her. What's your name?"

"Emma Shepherdson."

"Where do you live, Emma?"

Emma led her outside and pointed out the house. "Tell your mother we'll be happy to come after the children's meeting tomorrow night. Thank you, Emma."

Emma delivered the message to Ma, and all the next day she thought about it at school. She liked having company come to their house, but that Priscilla Johnston with her long dark curls? She wasn't so sure.

After the children's meeting, Emma rode with Johnstons in their buggy. She was glad for the ride even if she did have to share a seat with Priscilla.

Vina met them as they stepped out of the buggy. "Come on in," she said. "I'm Vina. By the time Pa and the boys finish the chores, we'll be ready." Vina led the mother and daughter into the house. "Emma, why don't you show the little girl your doll?"

Emma still didn't like Priscilla very much, but she had to be polite to her guest. She took her to the bedroom where she had her doll in a little bed Lester had made for her. "Is that the only doll you have?" Priscilla asked. "My doll's bigger than that."

Emma picked up her doll and held her close. "She's my Myrtle, and I love her."

Just then Ma called, "Come, Emma, and wash your hands for supper. Show Priscilla where to wash."

"Yes, Ma."Emma placed her doll back in the little bed.

She was glad it was time for supper. She didn't want to play with that girl. "Here's the sink, Priscilla."

They went to the table where the others were taking their places, and all bowed their heads while Pa asked the blessing on the food. The table was spread with a red and white checked tablecloth. Ma passed the platter of ham to Mrs. Johnston.

"My, that looks good. Do you cure your own ham?"

"Yes, we do," Pa said, and he told them about the little smokehouse in the back yard where they hung their hams and bacon when they butchered a hog.

It was a good supper. Ham was Emma's favorite, and the meal was finished off with some of Ma's delicious sugar cookies.

The Johnstons gave the Shepherdsons a picture of their

family.One day after the Crusaders had left the area, and when no one was looking, Emma went quietly into the parlor, picked up the picture from the parlor table, and scratched the pretty little girl's face with a pin.

"So there!" she said.

Chapter 3

Emma would probably be punished for scratching "that girl's" picture, but she didn't care.Priscilla was rude, she with her pretty face and brown curls!

The parlor was not used very often, so it was several days before Ma discovered the marred picture and asked Emma, "Do you know how this picture of the Johnstons got scratched?It looks like someone deliberately scratched the little girl's face."

"Yes, Ma, I did it," Emma said, relieved that she didn't have to hide her dark secret any longer.

"Why, Emma, why did you ever do such a thing?They were such nice people."

"Well, Priscilla wasn't nice to me.She asked me if Myrtle was the only doll I had, and she said her doll was bigger.I don't want her to come back here, and I don't want her to play with Myrtle."Emma wiped her eyes on her sleeve.

"It does sound like she wasn't very nice to you, but that was not a reason for you to spoil her picture.Don't ever do a thing like that again, Emma!"

"I won't, Ma," and Emma wiped her eyes again.

"Here comes Pa with Lena," Ma said, her face brightening.

"Lena's home, Lena's home," Emma chanted.Suddenly she felt much happier.The ordeal about the picture was over.Ma had seemed to understand how she felt about that girl.

Lena came in carrying a valise."How's Emma?" she asked, hugging her little sister.

"I'm fine except for that big bully at school that laughs at me and calls me 'Squinty Eyes.'"

"That's really mean of him, Emma.I'm sorry to hear that."

"How was your week at school?"Ma asked her oldest daughter.

"It was all right.I think it'll be easier this year."

Ma didn't even seem to hear what Emma had said.Leroy Sanders called her "Squinty Eyes" because she had to walk up to the blackboard to read what it said.What she said didn't seem to matter.She wasn't pretty like Pearl, and she had weak blue eyes instead of brown ones, "dishwater blond" hair instead of auburn like all her sisters.

"Don't forget you'll be having more pupils when the big boys come in after harvest," Ma reminded Lena.

"Yes, I know, but at least I've done it one year, so I know I can do it.It'll be a little easier."

Vina came in with a basket full of eggs."Lena, you're home," she said, and the high pompadours bumped as the sisters exchanged hugs.

"Hello," Lena greeted Pa and the boys as they came in from the barn.

After a quick greeting the boys headed for the basement door with their pails of warm milk.

After they had strained the milk and stored it in pans in the meat safe, they bounded up the steps, two at a time, to the kitchen to wash at the sink and prepare for supper.

Lester combed his curly brown hair at the mirror in the dining room.Then he pulled Vina's apron string hard enough to untie it as he chanted,"Vina's got a beau, and I know his name."

"Oh, Lester, go away.Leave my apron alone, and what if I do have a beau?Orville's a nice boy."

"Is he coming over tonight?" Lester asked.

"No, not until tomorrow night.We're going to the Christian Endeavor party at Popps's house.You're going too, aren't you?"

"Yes, I plan to,"Lester said, "but I don't have a girl to take."

"Well, that's not my fault," Vina laughed."Besides you're young.You have plenty of time for girlfriends.George, are you going to the C.E. party tomorrow?"

"Yes, I want to.Blondie, Blondie, Emma is a blondie!"He gave a playful tug at one of her braids.

"George, don't pull my hair!"Emma cried and hit him on the back.I'd rather be a blondie than a blackhead like you!"

"Come now, both of you," Pa ordered."Sit down and calm down, so we can pray.Dear Heavenly Father, we thank you for our family, our six healthy children.We thank you for the bountiful meal we are about to enjoy.Help us to eat with grateful hearts.In Jesus name, Amen."

After the girls had washed the supper dishes, and Emma had put the black-handled tableware away, Pa brought a game of Dominoes to the dining table."Lena, are you going to play Dominoes with us?" he asked.

"I'll play one game.Then I have to do some embroidery on a dress for Pearl.She's such a pretty baby, and she's laughing and 'talking' more all the time."Lena handed Pearl back to Ma.Ma would sit nearby, as usual, while her family played games.She would hold Pearl and be close enough to watch the progress of the game.Pearl's brown eyes sparkled, and her arms and legs seemed to be in perpetual motion.

"When are you going to make a dress for <u>me</u>, Lena?" Emma asked.

"As soon as I finish this one for Pearl."

After Lester won the first game of Dominoes, George left and brought a granite bowl full of beautiful red apples from the basement.

Taking an apple, Vina asked, "Lester, do you remember when Pa had typhoid fever?"

"Yes, I guess I do," he said as he turned Dominoes over for the next game. "Emmy was a baby and went to stay with Aunt Nancy and Uncle Milo.I was ten, and you must have been thirteen."

"Pa was so sick he wasn't able to do the spring plowing," Vina said.

"And you and I did it," Lester said. "I drove the horse, and you drove the plow."

"Those were hard times," Ma added. We ate lots of corn-meal mush and Johnny cake."

"Yes," Lester said, "I don't care if I <u>never</u> see any more cornmeal mush."

"And I hope I'm never that sick again," Pa said, "till I die. I wouldn't wish typhoid fever on anyone."

George began to laugh. "Pa, I'm not laughing at you.I was just laughing about the time you thought Lester had hurt me. I must have been about five and Lester eight. You came from the barn and saw us both standing near the windmill. I was crying,and Lester was laughing. You grabbed Lester and gave him a few good swats. Then you turned to me and asked, 'Now, young man, why are you crying?'

"I said, 'I-I-I th-th-threw a s-s-s-stone up in the air, and it c-came d-d-down and h-h-hit me on top of the head.'" They all laughed.

Pa smiled at the memory, "Yes, Lester, you got it that time instead of sometime when you should've had it and didn't get caught."

Next morning after a breakfast of fluffy pancakes, home-made maple syrup, and crisp side pork, the family remained at the table while Pa read from the "Sermon on the Mount" from his well-worn Bible. When he had finished reading, they all pushed back their chairs and knelt beside them while Pa prayed. He prayed for his family as well as neighbors and friends with special needs, and he prayed for the church. Actually he and Ma belonged to the Elbridge Methodist Church over several sand hills to the east, but since the Sackrider United Brethren Church was close, that's where they attended.

After family worship, George, Lester, and Pa left to work at the barn.Ma cared for Pearl while Vina was baking and Lena was cleaning the house, sweeping the hand-loomed rag carpet with a broom Pa had made on his broom machine with broom cane he had raised.

Emma didn't like dusting, but she knew she had to do it well, or Ma or Lena would make her do it over. As she was shaking her dust cloth outside the back door, their big part-collie dog Cub greeted her with wagging tail, a smile, and a handshake. She smoothed his fur and picked out a thistle burr. "Good dog, Cub." She also took time to pet Tiger Shep and his family before returning to her job.

By noon the morning chores were done, and the aromas from the kitchen called the family for dinner.

In the afternoon Vina pressed the dress she would wear to the party that night, a rose-sprigged muslin with pinafore ruffles over the shoulders.

Emma watched Vina comb her beautiful auburn hair. She put the hair she removed from the comb into a small china hair receiver with matching lid. She used this hair to form a "rat." Next she backcombed her hair on top." Doesn't it hurt when you comb out those snarls?" Emma asked.

"Yes, but it's the style. It helps the hair stand up for a nice pompadour," Vina replied. Then she shaped the "rat" in her hands, and laid it on the dresser. She swung her head down and brushed the front smooth. This done, she stood erect, set the rat on top of her head, and made an impressive pouf over the "rat" at the front with a smooth bun high on the back of her head.

The mantel clock on the shelf in the dining room was just striking seven when Orville Hobby's horse and buggy turned in at the Shepherdson driveway.

Chapter 4

Emma ran to open the door for Orville when he knocked. He held his hat and straightened his tie as she invited him in. She'd be happy when she could have a boyfriend.

Pa motioned for him to take the rocker near himself. "Good evenin,' Orville. How are you?"

"I'm fine, sir, and how are you?"

"Fair to middlin'. How's your farm work comin'? Have you harvested all your corn?"

"No, but we're workin' at it. If good weather holds, we should be able to finish up next week."

Orville smiled as Vina opened the stair door. She was lovely.

"Hello, Orville," she greeted, smiling. "Sorry to keep you waiting."

"We've got plenty of time. Is anyone else going to the party?"

"Yes," Lester spoke up. "We'll drive our own buggy and see you there."

"All right, Vina, shall we go?"

"Yes," she said, tucking a white shawl under her arm.

Soon Lester and George left for the party too. Emma wished she could go. "Ma, when will I be able to go to

Christian Endeavor parties?"

"When you're twelve," Ma replied. "George just started going this year."

"How about a game of checkers, Em?" Pa asked.

She loved having Pa call her "Em." That was his special name for her. "All right, Pa. Maybe I can beat you this time."

As they were riding home from church the next day, George said, "Vina, I bet you liked Sly Winkum best of all the games last night. Frank Hoffmyer kept trying to get you away from Orville, and Orville kept winkin' you back to his chair."

"Yes, that was fun," and she laughed, turning toward Lester. "You really enjoyed the lap supper, didn't you?"

"Well, I couldn't decide which was better, the sandwiches or the cake, so I had first one and then the other.I was just testing them."

"Lester, I hope you didn't make a pig of yourself at Mrs. Popp's house," Ma scolded.

"Oh, no, Ma.Mrs. Popp said, 'Eat all you want, and pocket none.' What I want to know, Vina, is if Orville kissed you."

"It's really none of your business, Nosey, but, no, he didn't kiss me. He just held my hand."

Cub, the family dog, was scratching at the back door for attention. He had some interesting habits. He would sometimes go away and stay for a week, even a month. When he returned he seemed happy to see the whole family and shook hands all around.

Pa tired of having a dog that didn't stay home, so one day he brought home a short-haired terrier puppy. The children each submitted a name for him, agreeing that the one Pa drew from a hat would be the puppy's name. Emma wrote "Sport" on her slip, and that was the one drawn. Some of her siblings didn't like the name, but Pa held them to their agreement, so the dog was Sport, and they all loved him, but

Emma most of all.

She was happy when winter came. She loved to roll down the snow banks near her house. Over and over she rolled, her red flannel bloomers making a vivid contrast to the pure white snow.

When she was tired and cold, she trudged home.Ma met her at the back door and swept the snow off from her with a broom. "Go stand by the stove and dry your stockings and your long underwear. Turn around with your back to the stove and pull up your skirts to dry out your bloomers. No one is around to see you. If you don't get dried out, you'll catch your death of cold."

At school she enjoyed sledding with her friends at recess and noon. "Play time! Play time! Bernice, let's go sliding on the hill. I brought my sled today. Did you bring yours?"

"I sure did," Bernice Eisenlohr replied. "Let's hurry, so we can get to the hill before John Campbell does."

"Yes, let's.He's so mean," Emma said, tying her gray Klondike bonnet under her chin. She flipped her braids out from her warm coat and buttoned it. "Let's go get our sleds," she called, starting out the door.

"I'm coming, Emma. Wait for me," Bernice cried. I can't get my overshoe on. Can you help me?"

"Sure. I'll push, and you pull. There you go. Now let's go. Maybe John Campbell is already out on the hill!"

Outside the school, they faced a cold wind as they untied their sleds from the icy pipe rail of the porch. Out to the road they ran with their sleds. The road was not very busy, and it was a wonderful hill for sledding. They could sometimes slide an eighth of a mile.

They sat on their homemade sleds at the top of the hill, holding the ropes they would use for steering. "Lucile, will you give us a push?" Emma called to their friend.

"All right. You can give me a push next time." Lucile said as she pushed first Emma and then Bernice to help them start down the hill.

"Whee!" Emma called with glee, as she went faster and faster down the icy hill. "This is so much fun!"

"Yes, this is fun," yelled John Campbell, one of the big eighth graders, as he rammed Emma's sled with his to slow it down. Then he grabbed the rope out of her hands and jerked the sled out from under her. She went flying off her sled, scraping her chin on the ice.

"John Campbell, you're a hateful boy!" she cried, picking herself up and wiping blood from her chin. Tears mixed with the blood on her face and on her mitten. "Why are you so mean to us little kids?"

"Cry baby! Cry baby!" John yelled without mercy, as he threw her sled into the snow bank beside the road.

"Now I have to go all the way back to the top of the hill to start over," Emma wailed. As she turned to climb the hill, she saw Bernice sailing smoothly over the icy road near the bottom of the hill.

The next morning as Emma was walking to school, a man driving a two-horse sleigh stopped to offer her a ride. She hopped up into the sleigh, glad for the ride, even with a neighbor she didn't know.

The man said, "I hear you have a new preacher at the church."

"Yes, we do. His name is Rev. Campbell."

"Oh, is that so?" the man asked. Any relation to the Campbells that live around here?

"No, I don't think so."

"What kind of boys are those Campbell boys?"

"Oh, Crate's all right, but John's a terror."

"What does John do?"

"He jerks the sleds out from under us little kids!" she said loudly, pointing to her scraped chin. He did it to me just yesterday."

The next day at school, Creighton Campbell said as he

came near Emma, "Crate's all right, but John's a terror."

"Who told you that?" Emma asked, turning red.

"My father," Crate said. "He gave you a ride to school in the sleigh. He told us what you said about us."

"Oh, no!" Emma choked, covering her face with her hands. "What happened? What did your pa say?"

"John got a good talking to. Pa told him that if her ever hears of him bullying the little kids again, he'll give him a good thrashin,'" Crate replied.

"Oh, I'm glad!" Emma burst out." Now maybe he'll leave us alone. Wait 'till I tell Bernice!"

Chapter 5

Frank Hoffmyer eventually succeeded in winning Vina away from Orville. She was dating Frank the winter of 1902, the year of the "Big Revival."

He came for her with his shiny red cutter on Sunday night, the opening night of the revival. Vina was wearing a dark blue wool dress with leg-of-mutton sleeves when she met him at the door. "Good evening, Frank.Come in," she greeted.

"Good evenin', yourself. You're lookin' mighty nice tonight. Are you ready to go?"

"All ready but my coat, hat and overshoes. Take a seat. I'll only be a minute." She showed Frank into the dining room where Pa was sitting by the round-oak stove.

"Good evenin', Mr. Shepherdson. Are you goin' to church tonight?"

"No, I don't think so. I went this mornin' though. We all did. Rev. Schultz is the new pastor. He's a fiery one. He used to be a blacksmith up to Walkerville."

"Oh, is that so? Does he still live up there?"

"No, he and his family have moved into the parsonage by the church in Hart, the other church on the circuit. Like I said, he used to be a blacksmith, and he sorta shakes people over the fire of hell. You won't go to sleep. At the same time, he tells them of a loving Jesus who is holding out His hand to rescue them."

"I'm ready when you are, Frank," Vina announced.

"All right.Good evenin', Sir.Good evenin', Mrs. Shepherdson. "Frank took his hat in one hand and Vina's elbow in the other.

Emma watched from the kitchen window as Frank helped Vina into the cutter. The front curved up gracefully and curled over, and the runners shone in the light from the window. Frank gave his dappled gray horse a signal, and the cutter glided over the snow and out of sight.

"Ma, can I go to church tonight?" Emma asked.

"No, not tonight. Maybe tomorrow night you can go with the others."

Lester and George came downstairs dressed for church. "We'll see you," Lester said as they left on foot.

"All right," Pa said, as he unfolded the *GRAND RAPIDS PRESS*.

"Emma, read 'tory," Pearl coaxed.

Emma picked up the toddler and set her on the spindle couch beside her. "All right, Pearly, here's a story from my Sunday School paper, the story of 'Daniel in the Lion's Den.' "

Ma was reading *UNCLE TOM'S CABIN*. She didn't sew or knit on Sunday.

"Em, when you get Daniel out of the lion's den, would you please go down cellar and bring up a pan of apples?"

"Sure, Pa," and she went on reading.

When she finished the story and started for the cellar, Pearl cried, "More, more!"

"No, my dear," Ma said, putting down her book. "It's time for our little Pearl to go to bed."

"More 'tory, more 'tory!" she cried.

"Not tonight, Pearl, maybe tomorrow," Ma said as she scooped her up and off to bed.

Emma brought a granite bowl full of jonathan apples from the cellar. The boys would want some when they came home from church, too.

Pa took out his cud of tobacco and placed it on the edge of the wainscoting before reaching for an apple. "Thank you, Em."

"Pa, why did Pap Gring wave his hanky in church today?"

"He always does that when he gets blessed, Em. He waves his hanky and sings 'Pass Me Not, O Gentle Savior.' He's just praising the Lord."

"He always sings the same song, doesn't he?"

"Yes, he does.Pap Gring is as well acquainted with the Lord as anyone in church. When he prays, he really gets hold of heaven."

"He prays awful loud."

"Pap Gring cares deeply about his neighbors, and he wants them all to know the Lord."

Emma had to go to bed before the boys and Vina came home from church, but she heard the boys come. She knelt down by the stovepipe in her room. If she put her ear down by the grating around the pipe, she could hear some of the conversation. Lester and George were both talking at once. "The sermon was really good, Pa," George said.

"And long," Lester interrupted.

"And a lot of people went to the altar to get saved!" George said.

"Did you come straight home from church?" Pa asked. "It's ten o'clock."

"Yes, Pa, we did," Lester answered. Vina and Frank turned west when they left the church, so they'll be home later."

The next night Lester helped Vina and Emma into the

sleigh while George held the reins of the horses. The sleigh was like a big bobsled with a huge box on it. They huddled together in the straw for warmth. When Lester had hopped up into the sleigh, he took the reins from George and said, "Giddy up." When they reached the church, the girls jumped down from the sleigh and brushed straw from their clothes. The boys took the horses into the horse shed and tied them securely.

When the invitation was given at the close of the message, George went forward to receive Christ.

The next night when Pastor Schultz asked for testimonies, George stood up. "I want to thank you folks, especially Pap Gring, for praying for me. Last night I asked Jesus to forgive my sins and make me His child, and I've never been so happy in my life. I feel all clean inside."

"Praise God from whom all blessings flow!" Pap Gring shouted.

Jessie Harwood decided to come out from Hart and take in one of the services. The third night he attended he made his way to the altar and made peace with God. He talked to his brothers about it, encouraging them to seek the peace of Jesus in their hearts.

The next night Frank Harwood and Vina were among the "seekers." When Frank gave his testimony, he said, smoothing his blond hair, "When we lived up North at Prentice Bay, where Pa worked in the logging business, I had a bad reputation. I was younger then, but I was a real nuisance around the sawmill. They gave me the nickname of 'the white-haired devil.'" Tonight I asked the Lord to forgive me and start me out with a clean slate."

Harry Harwood, the youngest of Uncle Silas and Aunt Tip's boys, knelt at the altar the following night. Neither of their parents was able to be there to see their boys coming to the Lord, three of the four, so far.

The night Charlie Harwood went forward he prayed for

a long time at the altar, but he did not come up smiling as all the others did.Something was troubling him.

The next night Charlie, better known as Chub, was at the altar again as soon as the invitation was given. He had hardly knelt when he jumped up, shouting, "Hallelujah! Thank you, Jesus, for washing my heart and forgiving me! Now I know I'm saved."

Pastor Schultz knew it was time for a testimony. "Chub, why don't you tell us what happened? We know you were not satisfied last night, even though you prayed for a long time."

"Pastor," Chub began, "last night when I was trying to get God to forgive my sins, all I could see was a pitchfork, yes, a pitchfork! I knew what I had to do.

"Last fall I was driving the horse on Jake Trommater's farm, where I work, pulling a load of potatoes on the stone boat. Jack is sometimes a balky horse, and he went back when I told him to go forward. I whacked him across the rump with the pitchfork I'd been usin' to dig the potatoes. I hit 'im so hard that I broke the handle of the pitchfork. Mr. Trommater wasn't around, so I hid the broken pitchfork instead of telling him about it.

"Last night when I left church, I knew I had to make that right. I went home and borrowed two dollars from my brother Frank. This morning I went to Mr. Trommater and told him the story, offering him the money for the pitchfork.

"He said, 'Well, Charlie, I guess if the Lord can forgive you, I can too. Keep your two dollars.'

"When I went back to the altar tonight, immediately the Lord touched me. It was like a bolt of lightning touched me on the head, and the heat flowed through my body. Hallelujah!" he shouted as the tears rolled down his cheeks, and he sat down. The revival services went on for three weeks. Pa called it "the Big Revival."

Pap Gring, not one to miss an opportunity, took George

to preach at the Randall School on Sunday afternoons. The school services did not have a regular preacher, but the fourteen-year-old filled the position for a time, declaring his new-found faith.

Soon Shepherdsons were into the maple syrup season. Cub reappeared after a month's absence, shook hands all around, and enjoyed making the rounds of the sugar bush.

Emma could hardly wait until Ma decided the weather was warm enough to go barefoot. Cousins Bess and Gladys Waterman were coming out from Hart to spend some time on the farm. Bess was three years older than Emma, and Gladys three years older than Pearl.

The week the girls arrived, Ma made a pink chambray dress for Emma, and a navy print one for Bess, the same style as Emma's.

It was a standing rule that the girls were to wash the dishes after breakfast while Ma went to work in the garden. The two girls, basking in the pleasure of the new dresses, dashed off for a visit with Aunt Tip, without washing the dishes. They stayed a long time, but Ma wouldn't punish Emma because Cousin Bess was with her, would she?

Ma was waiting for the girls with an apple switch when they returned from visiting Aunt Tip.Emma howled as Ma switched her back and shoulders. After a few good strokes, Ma let Emma go and started on Bess, her namesake. Bess was older, more stoic, and wouldn't cry, so she received more strokes than Emma.

Chapter 6

Cousin Jessie Harwood noticed Emma walking up to the blackboard to copy her assignments because of poor vision.He was their new teacher when Emma was in fourth grade.

"Uncle Charlie," he said, "Emma needs glasses. She has to stand very close to the black board to copy her assignments."

"Well," Pa said, "I guess we'd better have her eyes tested.I wonder why she never said anything about it or her teachers either."

"I don't know, but she surely needs glasses. She's a good student, but she's working at a disadvantage."

"We'll see to it right away," Pa said, and he did. In a few weeks Emma was wearing glasses and called "Four Eyes" by some older boys, and her self esteem took another tumble. Unfortunately those first glasses didn't help much.She still had to walk up to the board to read her assignments, so Pa took her to another doctor. The next pair of glasses were much better.

Mr. Harwood's teaching was fascinating to Emma as well as the other children. The whole school enjoyed his learning games. For the primary children he drew a ladder on the board with a word on each rung. As the child succeeded in reading each word, he would go up the ladder.If he missed, he fell down into the straw.

For the older children, Friday afternoon was a time for geography downs, spell downs, or cipher downs. Emma loved competition, and she did well in these games.

Her running skill was used at school during play time. She and Lucile were two of the fastest runners, so they were chosen to be the fire team to pull the make-believe fire engine, driven by Lloyd Newberry.

Ma had told her that she must not go to Aunt Lucy's general store three-quarters of a mile west of the school during lunch hour unless Ma had sent her for something.

One day Bernice said, "Emma, Ma sent me to the store today. Will you go with me?"

"Oh, no, Ma said not to go unless she sends me," Emma replied.

"But I don't want to go alone. Please just this once?" Bernice pleaded.

"Oh, all right, just this once," Emma gave in, "but we'll have to hurry, or we'll be late for school. Let's run."

It was easy running downhill past the church on the right, Freeborns' farm, then the Monroe Thomas place. Going uphill wasn't so easy.They could see the store now. Aunt Lucy and Uncle Perl's house was up on a hill with a long driveway, but the store and Tigris Post Office were down next to the road, across from McDonalds' blacksmith shop.

They were out of breath by the time they reached the store. Everything was available from cloth to crackers, cheese in large round chunks under a round glass lid, stick candy, and kegs of nails, among other things. The telephone exchange and Post Office were in one corner. Emma looked at as many things as possible while Bernice did her mother's shopping. As soon as Bernice was ready, Emma greeted Aunt Lucy, and the girls hurried out the door.

Down the steps of the porch they ran, past an apple orchard on the right, past Grandpa and Grandma Ridge's cedar swamp. Emma loved to go there and drink water from the bubbling spring, but not today. On they ran, slowing down to a walk as they climbed the hill near the school.

When Emma arrived home after school, Ma asked, "Did you go to the store today, Emma?"

"No, Ma."

"Now, Emma, are you telling me the truth?"

"Yes, Ma," she said again, becoming very uncomfortable.

"Emma, you can't be telling the truth, because Lester was at the blacksmith shop, and he saw you and Bernice coming out of the store."

Emma started crying. "Yes, Ma, I did go to the store with Bernice. She had to go for her mother, and she didn't want to go alone. She wanted me to go with her."

"Why did you lie to me, Emma?"

"Because you told me not to go to the store. I'm sorry, Ma."

" 'What a tangled web we weave when first we practice to deceive,' " Ma quoted an old saying. "Don't ever lie to me again, Emma. I want to be able to trust you."

"You can trust me, Ma," she sobbed. "I won't lie to you again." She went to her room and flung herself across her bed and cried. She wanted Ma to be able to trust her. She was sorry she had disappointed her.

Ma was the oldest of Grandpa Ridge's five daughters, and Uncle Wesley was the youngest child, and only son. The daughters were all married, but Uncle Wes was a young man living at home at the time.

Grandpa was talking with Pa one day, and Emma overheard the conversation, "Wesley has worked for James Smith all summer, and he hasn't been paid for the last six weeks."

"Has Wesley asked him about it?"

"Yes, and so have I. In fact, I just came from his place. I

asked him about it in a civil way, and he told me he'd pay Wes when he got good and ready. Then he told me to get off his property. I'm so riled up, I don't know what to do!"

The next day at school Emma found out what he did. Inez Smith confronted her on the road as she was arriving, "Your grandpa shot my grandpa!" she shouted, so all the children in the school yard could hear.

"He did not!" Emma defended.

"He did so!" Inez shot back." I saw the big bandage on his leg, and it was all bloody!"

"My grandpa wouldn't do a thing like that!" Emma cried.

"Well, he did, and he's in jail right now! He came right up to my grandpa's farm yesterday, and shot him for no reason," Inez yelled.

"In jail?" Emma wailed.She wondered if it could be possible.Grandpa couldn't be in jail. She'd seen him only yesterday. She knew he was very angry. "Well, he did have a reason. Your grandpa didn't pay Uncle Wesley for six weeks of hard work on the farm. Uncle Wesley asked him about it, and Grandpa talked to him nicely about it. He told Grandpa he'd pay Uncle Wes when he got good and ready. So I guess he did have a reason!"

A crowd had gathered outside the school by that time. Harvey Slate said, "My pa was at the blacksmith shop, and he heard Mr. Ridge tellin' about Mr. Smith not payin' Wesley. Manley Smith was in the blacksmith shop at the time. He must have had problems with his father too. He said, 'Why don't you shoot the old man?' So I guess that's what he did. He took a shotgun and shot 'im in the leg."

"I saw Mr. Ridge when he was drivin' his buggy past our house. He was drivin' like Jehu!" Nathan Tate said.

"Well, no matter what the reason was, Emma's grandpa had no business shootin' my grandpa!" Inez had the last word as the bell rang, and they all ran into the school.

Emma's heart was pounding, and she had to keep using

her handkerchief to dab at her eyes and nose. Was it really true? She couldn't believe it yet. Maybe it was all a dream, a very bad dream. She pinched herself. Yes, she was truly awake. Her eyes were open. She wondered if Grandpa really was in jail.

Chapter 7

Grandpa Ridge was truly in jail! What a sad day for Emma's family! In due course he was tried and sent to the Michigan State Prison in Ionia.

Though Emma had had nothing to do with the incident, she was in disgrace at school. James Smith's injury was not serious. Still, Grandpa had taken the law into his own hands, and he and his family suffered the consequences.

Emma now had mixed feelings about going to school. Sometimes it was unpleasant. She was the only one from her family at Sackrider School at that time. Vina had passed her State Teacher's Exam and was teaching at the Randall School. Lester and George had both graduated from eighth grade, so Emma had to bear the shame alone.

Aunt Nancy, who lived in the Cedar community, northeast of Shepherdsons, could not stand to go to church and meet people's accusing looks. Her father had shot a man. Lena was now teaching the Cedar School and boarding with Aunt Nancy.

Emma went with Pa to fetch Lena from Aunt Nancy's house one Friday. "How are you, Nancy?" Pa greeted.

"I'm pretty fair. I've had a very busy week. Monday night I was called out to deliver a baby, yesterday to care for a sow with piglets. I was showing Lena an unusual payment for three weeks of home nursing. She left and reappeared with a large, scalloped, china fruit dish. "I had taken care of Mrs. Carmony for three weeks when she was ailing. When she was better, and I was getting ready to leave, her husband said, 'We ain't got no money. Would you take this here pretty dish fer yer payment?' Of course I said I would."

At home Emma was becoming a skillful little seamstress. Ma had started her sewing on a nine-patch quilt for Myrtle. Now she was making clothes for the doll. When one of her older sisters was cleaning the house and would come across Emma's doll clothes she had made, they would say, "Emma, come pick up your doll's rags."

"They are not rags!" she protested as she ran to rescue them and put them away.

Soon she was sewing for others. Lewie Hull, a little neighbor boy, had broken his leg in a sledding accident. It was very difficult for the active boy to be confined to bed with a cast on his leg. His family had a baby-size doll, which he played with, so Emma made new clothes for the doll to help entertain the child.

One night Emma's second cousin Maude Rummer came to stay overnight. Sometimes Lena let Emma play with her pretty doll with a china head, and Emma was very careful with it. She took Lena's doll to play with while Maude was there, and Maude broke the doll. Emma cried. She felt responsible for her sister's lovely doll, but she was not punished when it was broken.

Next morning when Emma and Maude were called for breakfast, Emma ignored the call and stayed in bed, taking advantage of having a guest. When the girls did go downstairs, Pa stood with his foot up on the woodbox and a slipper in his hand.Emma understood. She bent over his knee, and he paddled her with the slipper.

When Lena came home for Christmas vacation, she took

Emma with the horse and cutter to the store to buy cloth for a new dress for her. Aunt Lucy always had new and interesting things in the store. This time a beautiful pair of dolls captured her attention. One had brown hair and brown eyes with a red felt body and the other blond hair, blue eyes, and a blue body. They were beautiful dolls with real hair and eyes that opened and closed.

As she was taking in all the details of the dolls in the glass case, Aunt Lucy noticed. "Those dolls are spoken for, Emma." Emma's heart fell. She would so love to have the one with a red body and brown hair.

Lena looked at cloth, and Emma was delighted when Lena chose a red plaid with a dark green stripe and some white eyelet edging for trim. "Oh, yes, Ma needs five pounds of sugar and a can of molasses. I was thinking about some of that cheese too. Could I taste a sample of it?"

"Sure thing," Aunt lucy replied, lifting the big glass lid and slicing off a sliver for Lena to taste.

"That's fine," she said after tasting it, and sharing it with Emma. "We'll take a pound of that."

Lena carried most of their purchases in a basket she'd brought along.Emma was delighted to carry her cloth and think of a pretty new dress, a red one. Usually Ma made red dresses for Pearl and blue ones for Emma. She had a last longing look at the beautiful dolls, especially the red one, as she and Lena tied their bonnet strings and pulled on warm mittens before stepping outside into the cold. Emma hopped into the cutter as Lena untied the reins from the hitching post, climbed in and gave the signal to their horse Pet. They covered their laps with a warm buffalo robe and were on their way home.

"Lena, did you know that Jessie and Sadie are going to put up a Christmas tree?" Emma asked as they were riding along.

"No, I didn't, but that sounds lovely. I saw one once. It

was decorated with strings of popcorn and all kinds of pretty things."

"I've never seen one," Emma said. "It must be nice. I can't wait to see it. They've invited us to their house for Christmas Eve. Won't that be fun?"

"Yes, it will. I'll look forward to that too."

Jessie Harwood and Sadie Trull had married in Hart a few years before, and that year the couple and their baby Anna were living with Aunt Tip and caring for her while Uncle Silas was away, working in the logging camp. It was great to have them for neighbors.Pearl and Emma enjoyed going over and playing with Baby Anna.

"Lena, do you know what I'm making for Anna for Christmas?"

"No, what are you making?"

"A pair of white panties.I'll show you when we get home."

"I'd like to see them."

As soon as they arrived at home, Emma pulled off her warm wraps and took out her latest sewing project to show Lena. "See, aren't they going to be nice?"

"Yes, but they're too big, don't you think so, Vina?"

"Yes, I tried to tell her that."

"Do you really think I should make them smaller?" Emma asked.

Both sisters thought so.Emma found the scissors and trimmed the panties around the edges, cutting off seams she had already sewn except the top. She would have to start all over again, almost. She threaded a needle, pinned the sides together, and started sewing them by hand. She'd have to work hard and fast to finish them by Christmas Eve, the very next night.

That evening she and Lena and Ma were all busy with their needles while the others played games.

Early the next morning Emma was working on her

project. As soon as she had washed the breakfast dishes, she took up her needle again. She and Vina did the dinner dishes together. Then Ma asked Emma to dust the furniture in the parlor.

"Ma, I'm not finished with Anna's panties!" she complained.

"You'll have time to do them after you dust the parlor," Ma said.

Emma jerked the dustcloth from its nail and hurried into the parlor, pouting, but determined to do the job quickly, so she could get back to her sewing. First she dusted the parlor lamp. She must not hurry too fast with that. The globe of the lamp was beautifully painted with pink roses on a pale green background. She quickly moved from the lamp to the table under it, gliding over the walnut surface and carved legs.

As soon as she'd finished the rest of the furniture, she took up her sewing again.

By four o'clock she was ready for Ma to help her with the elastic in the top of the panties. "My, but they look small, Emma," Ma commented.

"Lena and Vina said they were too big, so I cut them down. I hope they're big enough now."

"I hope so too," Ma said.

While Emma pressed and wrapped Anna's panties, she thought about the Christmas tree they would see at Harwoods' house, and she wondered if she would see those dolls again.

Chapter 8

Full of anticipation, Emma took her gift for Anna and joined the family as they walked across to Harwoods' house.

The Christmas tree was beautiful! Strings of popcorn and cranberries were draped gracefully around it. There were also crocheted snowflakes and a few bright-colored glass balls. On the very top was a thin yellow star made of wood. Emma and Pearl could hardly take their eyes off the tree and the packages under it.

After the adults had visited for a few minutes, Jessie said, "Now let's have a look under the tree. Emma, how would you like to be Santa Claus and pass out the gifts?"

"I'd love to!" she cried.

"Me help," Pearl offered.

"All right, Pearly you can help," Emma agreed."Here's one for Aunt Tip."Next Emma handed Anna the gift she had made for her. Anna tore the paper and hugged the panties to herself.

Then Emma turned her attention back to the job of handing out the rest of the gifts with Pearl's help until Pearl opened a package containing a small toy, which she enjoyed. After that, she left the rest of the gifts for Emma to deliver.One with Emma's name on it was a game of Authors.

She had never played the game, but she knew she would like it. She enjoyed games of any kind.

"Oh, no!" she wailed when she saw Sadie trying to put the panties on Anna. "They're too small!"

"They'd probably have been all right if her sisters had let her alone," Pa commented. They told her the panties were too big, so she cut them smaller. Sorry, Em, you'll have to make her another pair."

Except for the disappointment about her gift to Anna, Emma had a good time.Jessie showed them how to play Authors. It was fun. The object was to collect complete sets of each author's book titles, and the one who had the most sets won the game. She would treasure her Authors game.

As they were walking home, Emma thought, "No dolls under the Christmas tree."

Before they went to bed, she and Pearl hung their stockings on nails under the clock shelf, along with all the other members of the family, including Ma and Pa. Up the stairs they went and changed into their flannel nightgowns, hopping into bed, thinking about Christmas morning.

Early the next morning Emma was wakened by a rooster crowing. She jumped out of bed, and ran downstairs with Pearl right behind her. They opened the stair door, and ran across the dining room to their stockings. The dolls were there! They were looking out of the tops of the girls' stockings! The brunette was in Pearl's stocking, and the blond one was in Emma's. She was a little disappointed not to receive the brown-haired doll, but she did not say anything about that. She did have a beautiful new doll. Both girls hugged their dolls and danced around with glee.

"What will you name your doll, Em?" Pa asked, coming out of his room, buttoning his shirt.

"I think I'll name him Nathan, Pa," she replied, her eyes shining. "I'll have to make a shirt and pants for 'im, and a cap."

Pa laughed. "So you're going to make it into a boy doll?"

"Yes, Pa."

"And what about our little Pearly" What are you going to name your doll?" he asked as he picked up Pearl, doll and all.

"Bethel, Pa."

"Your doll is Bethel?"

"Yeth, Pa, Bethel," Pearl said and hugged the beautiful doll.

By that time, Lester and George came downstairs, trying to smooth their tousled hair with their hands. "Merry Christmas, Emma!" Lester said.What have you got there?"

"My new doll Nathan," she said smiling.

"Oh, it's Nathan, is it?" he asked laughing."Let's see what's in my stocking." He pulled out a pair of beautiful blue suspenders. "Jim dandy!" he said and pulled out an orange too.

George said, "Pearly, what have you got?"

"Bethel," she said, hugging the doll close.

"She's a beautiful doll. What's in mine? Red suspenders. Aren't they pretty?" George said, pulling them out of his stocking. "And a beautiful orange."

By this time, Ma came out of her room, fully dressed. "What's all the fuss about?" she asked, and they all showed their treasures.

"What's in your stocking, Ma?" George asked.

"There's a little box. Oh, it's a beautiful brooch! That'll be just right on my new winter dress. What's in your stocking, Pa?"

"A fine new leather wallet. It looks like it's hand-tooled. I can certainly make good use of that. My old one is almost in pieces. Someone must have noticed that." And he looked at Ma and smiled.

Lena appeared next from upstairs. "Merry Christmas, Lena!" they chorused.

"Wake up, Vina!" Lester yelled up the stairs. "You're missing all the fun."

"I'm coming," she called back.

Lena found a small box in her stocking, which she opened carefully as they all watched. "Oh, it's lovely!" she exclaimed. "A beautiful breast pin. It will be perfect at the throat of my pale green waist."

"Merry Christmas, everybody!" Vina greeted as they were looking at Lena's gift. She went to her stocking as they all greeted her. "New combs, just what I need. And they're beautiful ones, tortoise shell with rhinestones. Let me try them in my hair," she said as she stepped to the mirror over the small table in the dining room. They did look stunning in her auburn hair.

After breakfast Pa read the Christmas story from Luke in the Bible for their devotions. "Lena, would you like to read about the Wise Men from Matthew?" He handed her the Bible.

The Christmas story never grew old, though they heard it often.Emma loved to hear it again.

Soon after Christmas, Rev. Wildman, their new pastor, held revival meetings at the church. The first evening Emma dressed warmly and joined Lester, George, and Vina. They stepped out into the crisp snow to walk to church.Vina and George carried their Bibles. Their feet crunched in the snow as they walked. They could hear sleigh bells coming from all directions to the church on the corner for revival meeting. Probably others like themselves were also arriving on foot.

Warm, welcoming light shone across the snow from the windows of the church on the hill as they approached.

Rev. Wildman was a good preacher, though not as fiery as Rev. Schultz.Emma could not remember what he said, but the message was for her. When the invitation was given, she knelt to the left of center at the spindle altar rail. She was eleven, and she knew she needed the blood of Jesus to cover her sins, the lying, the jealousy, and all the rest. Vina knelt beside her and prayed, "Dear God, please help Emmy to be a good little girl." Peace washed over Emma's heart. She felt so clean and light. The burden of guilt was gone! She wiped her eyes, blew her nose, then stood and exchanged hugs with Vina.

"Pa, I went to the altar tonight," she burst out when she got home.

Pa said, "That's good, Em, very good," and Ma gave her a hug.

The next night Vina, Lester, George, and Emma went to church again. this time it was Lester's turn. The handsome young man with curly brown hair made his way to the altar of prayer. George was there beside him to encourage and pray for his big brother. After praying a while, Lester stood up and wiped his eyes. What a smile was on his face!

Rev. Wildman was a brick mason as well as a pastor, so in the spring Pa hired him to build a chimney for a furnace to be installed in the basement of their house. In preparation for the furnace, a large hole was cut in the dining-living room floor for a register. Ma placed a rug over the hole.

One day Ma sent Emma to bring the large,flowered lamp from the parlor. She came whistling from the parlor, carrying the lovely lamp, completely forgetting the hole in the floor.

Chapter 9

Who-o-osh! Down she went, carpet, lamp and all, through the hole to the cellar! When she realized what was happening, it had already happened. She was sitting on the sandy cellar floor, surrounded by broken glass, still holding the lamp that was no longer flowered.

"Emma! Emma! Are you hurt?" Ma called from the hole above the child's head. "Wait, don't move! I'll come down."

Emma was shaking glass out of her hair and clothes when Ma reached her. "Are you all right?"

"Yes, I think so," Emma grinned. "Ma, I'm so sorry about the lamp! I forgot the hole was there."

"Well, it's my fault as much as yours. I shouldn't have put the carpet over the hole. Then you would've seen it. I'm glad you're all right. I'll help you clean up this glass. Be careful that you don't get cut. It'll be hard to find all the pieces of glass in the sand, but it's a good thing for you that you had sand to land on instead of cement.

"Glory be, Emma! What happened?" Lester called, coming down the cellar steps, two at a time.

"I forgot about the hole in the floor, and I was carrying the parlor lamp out to Ma in the kitchen!"

"So you took a shortcut to the cellar!" Lester laughed as

he stopped to help pick up pieces of glass. "Are you going to feel like going to the Christian Endeavor party tonight at Mundts' house?"

"Oh, I'm all right. All I hurt was the lamp and my pride.I was well padded where I landed," she laughed.

That evening Emma and Lester walked across the field to Mundt's C.E. party.She was glad now that she was allowed to attend the parties, that she was not cheated out of this one.

At the party Bernice rushed up, "Emma, did you hear that Jay Van Brocklin's sick?"

"No, what's wrong with him?"

"They say it's typhoid fever. He's awful sick."

"His ma came to the house and helped my ma when Pearl was born. Jay is about Lester's age.I wonder if he knows about it." She hurried across the room to share the news with him.

Jay was ill for weeks, and then he died. Emma and her family attended Jay's funeral at the Sackrider Church. When she looked at his emaciated body in the casket, she caught her breath. Turning away, she stumbled to her seat. It had been some time since she'd seen Jay, and was shocked at how terrible he looked. Pearl and the rest of the family joined her in the long pew. Emma didn't know if she could stand it to sit there until the service was over. She chilled and felt sick all over.

She soon blocked the funeral out of her mind. She thought about Grandma Shepherdson's death. Since Emma was only three when Grandma had died, Pa had held her up to see Grandma.Memories of Grandma continued. She had given her a beautiful handchief box covered with pink silk and decorated with shells and multi-colored porcupine quills. Emma kept the treasured box on her dresser. Grandma had brought red flannel for the little dress Emma still had, stored away. Grandma Shepherdson also made beautiful crazy quilts with all kinds of pretty stitches, embroidery, and even painting on some of the blocks.

Other people had died. She had attended other funerals, but those people didn't look as bad as Jay. After the burial at Elbridge Cemetery, Emma talked to Lester about it. He was sad because Jay had been his friend, but he didn't seem to feel the same way about the funeral as Emma did. "You know Pa had the same sickness. He was very sick, but I'm so glad he's still with us," Lester said.

Emma determined never to attend another funeral.

News that Pa's cousins, the Greggs, were coming from Chicago cheered Emma. She helped with the housecleaning and other preparations for the visit. Pa met the Greggs, Cousin Jane and her son and daughter, at the train station in Hart. He brought them home in the two-seated buggy he had enhanced by adding a canopy with green fringe.

They drove in with a cloud of dust billowing behind them. How grandly these city folks were dressed! Cousin Mabel's hat was huge, the largest Emma had ever seen. Vina said Cousin George was debonair. Mabel, younger than her brother was in her twenties. One day during their visit the lovely Mabel gave Vina a lesson in tatting. During the instruction, Lester went out, whittled a wooden shuttle, found a piece of string, and tatted a circle, learning faster than his sister.

After a week of visiting relatives in the area, the cousins prepared to leave. Mabel gave Pearl a doll with golden hair, a white leather body, and a china head with teeth. Pearl stroked the silky dress and hugged her new doll, promptly naming her "Mabel." It was the most beautiful doll she'd ever seen.Waving and calling warm farewells, the cousins rode out of the driveway and down the road with Pa.

A week later Emma was pleased to receive a postcard picture of Washington, D.C. from George Gregg, thanking them for their hospitality and saying they had arrived home safely.

After the visit of the Greggs, Lena moved into a room she had arranged to rent at Cousin Charlie Riddell's house in Hart. After graduating from eighth grade and teaching several years on her Third Grade Certificate, she had decided to attend County Normal to further her education. Thinking it was a good time for him to attend Hart High School, Lester also rented a room at Riddells' house, and he and Lena shared housekeeping chores.

Mrs. Elsie Riddell's brother Guy Barnes came from Iowa for a visit during the time Lena and Lester were living with the family.Guy was attracted to Lena and dated her. When they visited the Shepherdson farm sometimes, Emma saw them both sitting in a hammock under an apple tree in the front yard. Would the time ever come for her to have a beau?

Vina's current beau was Gene Putney. Pearl named a treasured little china cat Gene in his honor.

New neighbors, the Perry family from Bloomington, Illinois, moved next door when the Grings moved to another house. Perrys' son Roy was a young adult, and their daughter Rosa was halfway between the ages of Emma and Pearl, so the three of them became good friends.

One day Pa reported that he saw Roy Perry smoking a pipe.Vina commented, "Well, if he smokes a pipe, that's enough for me."

However, one morning when Roy came to the Shepherdson house to call, Vina jumped out the pantry window because she didn't have her hair combed. She was teaching at the Randall School, walking from home in fall and spring, and boarding in the Randall community in the winter.

George had gone to Hart High School one year and worked in a restaurant.He couldn't stand the foul language of his fellow-workers, so he dropped out of school.He was studious and really wanted to further his education, so the following year he traveled to Huntington, Indiana, to attend the United Brethren Academy at Central College. One of the things he left behind was a beautiful little desk he had built.

When George had gone, Vina moved his desk into what had been the store room and fixed it up for a bedroom for herself, since it was heated by the new furnace.

One evening she participated in a shadow social. She prepared a beautiful box with fried chicken, bread rolls, spread with Ma's homemade butter and strawberry jam, beet pickles, and chocolate cake she had baked. A shadow social was something like a box social, and it generated excitement among everyone in the community.

Girls and ladies who had prepared box lunches would assemble behind sheets hung like curtains at the front of the stage in the school. One by one they would move forward in front of a lamp placed at the back of the stage, each showing her profile behind the sheet as her box was auctioned to the highest bidder.Young men jostled each other good naturedly, forcing up the bidding. Box socials and shadow socials were fun, and the money helped pay for maps and other school materials.

Recognizing Vina's profile, Roy Perry bought her box for a high price against two other bidders. He had been at the house often to see her, but he soon went back to Illinois to look for work.

That was an exciting year for Emma. She was in seventh grade, and the teacher was the much-loved Dema Cargill.Miss Cargill prepared her students, and had confidence that her seventh graders were ready to take the eighth grade examination with a little tutoring in the evenings. For some reason Emma couldn't understand, Pa did not give permission for her to attend the tutoring sessions, so she had to study "The Song of Hiawatha" among other things, on her own. She worried dreadfully that she was missing some of the instruction that she needed, but she did her best at home.

Suspense was building.Frank Miller, Charlie Hull, Nathan Tate, Lucile Hodges, Inez and Leroy Wolfe and others were preparing, along with Emma to take the important exam.

Before the big day Emma turned 13 in April.They all went to the Elbridge Town Hall to write the exam along with students from other schools in the township. It was a standardized examination, taken by students all over the State of Michigan. Another teacher came to administer the exam instead of Miss Cargill.

Students from the different schools were separated from their friends and spaced at intervals at long tables in the Town Hall. Emma felt like she had dragon flies in her stomach as she took her place between two strangers.

Examination papers were distributed, and the students were told to sign their papers and keep them closed. All waited for the signal to open them and begin.

Chapter 10

Two whole days they sat at those exams, covering English grammar, literature, math, geography, history, and civics.Emma found nothing unfamiliar in the exams. Sackrider students had been well prepared, and when the results were out, Frank Miller made the highest score in their school. Emma was a few tenths of a point behind him, and Charlie Hull was close behind her.

Eighth Grade Graduation ceremonies were held at Elbridge Town Hall. Since they had passed the Eighth Grade Examination, they were ready to graduate from eighth grade a year early. Frank Miller and Emma Shepherdson were asked to make speeches as the top two students from Sackrider school. While Frank was delivering his speech, Emma was nervously rehearsing her lines to herself, smoothing the skirt of the white dress Lena had made for her. Lena had helped her with the speech too. When Frank was finished, Emma was introduced. She walked up to the platform and made her parents proud as she made her presentation. She sat down with feelings of pride and great relief mingling in her heart.

Were these young teenagers ready to go away to high school? Hart was at least five miles away for these students, too far to walk. Academically they were ready, but so immature to rent rooms in town to attend high school.

Their parents held a meeting to discuss the matter. The consensus at the meeting was that a second room should be added to the school and a second teacher hired to teach high school subjects. The children would attend school here at home for two more years. By that time they would be more mature and ready to go into town to school.

A spacious second room was built onto the school that summer, ready for the students to start high school classes in September. However,when school opened, Emma and most of her classmates started school in the old schoolroom with Miss Dema Cargill as their teacher. The school board, which included Mr. Henry Miller, had decided the new room should be used for the elementary children with his daughter Ethel teaching them.

Along with the new curriculum came a growing interest in the opposite sex. The girls made lists of boys' names, arranging them in the order of their preference. The order changed from time to time, but Nathan Tate was a name that was often at the top. He was a very handsome boy.

Parties were becoming more interesting.Christian Endeavor parties and others included games like Sly Winkum. Boys would stand behind chairs where girls were seated in a circle. One chair would be empty. The boy behind the empty chair would wink at the girl of his choice to try to get her to move to his chair. The boy behind her chair would grab his girl by the shoulders to keep her from moving if he noticed her invitation to move. The boy with the empty chair would keep trying until he succeeded in finding a girl to move to his chair. Emma couldn't see well enough, even with glasses, to enjoy Sly Winkum.

Another popular game was "Sailing on the Ocean." Emma and her friends played that game one evening at Charlie Hull's home. The players sang the song:

"Sailing on the ocean, the tide rolls high
Waiting for a pretty girl to come by and by.
There's many a lass that I let pass
Because I wanted you, because I wanted you.
There's many a lass that I let pass
Because I wanted you."

At that point in the song the boy in the center of the circle of players would approach the girl of his choice and kiss her. She would then go to the center, and the song would change to:

"Waiting for a handsome boy to come by and by,
There's many a beau that I let go
Because I wanted you."

She would then kiss the boy of her choice, and he would go to the center.

After the games Charlie showed everyone his new gramophone that he'd bought from money earned as the school janitor. They all admired its large horn and the sound produced by a needle moving around the grooves on a flat disc that rotated on a turntable. While they ate their lap supper, Charlie played his favorite record, "Tying the Leaves So They Won't Come Down." It was a sad song about a dying girl.

"I'm tying the leaves so they won't come down
So Nellie won't go away.
For the best little girl in the whole wide world
Is lying so ill today."

When all the leaves were off the tree the girl would die. It was commonly believed that a person who was ill with "consumption" (tuberculosis) was likely to die in October when leaves were falling from the trees.

When Emma arrived home from the party, Vina had news of Roy. He had found a job with the Chicago, Burlington and Quincy Railroad, maintaining electric switches. Soon he and Vina had a steady flow of letters between them. She kept her letters in a secret compartment in George's little desk.

Emma discovered the letters there one day and found them oh, so interesting! Would she ever receive wonderful letters like that? Several days later after savoring the recent letters, she had to leave quickly when she heard Vina coming.

"Ma, Em's been into my letters!" Vina called.

"How do you know she has, Vina?"

"Because they weren't put back just the way I left them." She cried indignantly. "Emma, if I ever catch you reading my private mail again, I'll fix you good!"

Emma almost said, "I put them back very carefully, including the little board to the secret compartment." Then she decided that wouldn't help her, so she took the tongue lashing, which she deserved, and respected Vina's privacy.

Soon good news came in the form of Grandpa Ridge's early release from prison for good behavior. He came home to Grandma Eliza Ridge, who was Emma's Step Grandmother. She was very skilled in making hair wreaths. One Saturday when everyone was at home, she came to the house for hair samples for her work. She took some dark brown hairs from Ma and Pearl, black from George, auburn from Vina and Lena, brown from Pa and Lester, and strawberry blond from Emma. With these human hairs she formed beautiful flowers, using fine wire. With the same skill, she also made more colorful yarn wreaths. These were mounted in velvet-lined shadow boxes. Shepherdsons had one of her lovely yarn wreaths on their parlor wall.

In February when days began to get longer, Pa would take four helpers, usually his own boys and two others, to tap the maple trees. After drilling the holes, they inserted small metal tubes called spiles.

Sap ran best when days were sunny and warm and nights were cold. Tin buckets without handles were hooked onto the spiles to catch the sweet liquid.

Pa or one of the boys would drive the horses, pulling a long low wagon carrying a four-barrel tank. Buckets of sap were poured into the top of the tank through a screen to filter out leaves or sticks. The horses learned the route through the 25 acres of woods. They would not stop at the beech or oak trees, only the maple trees, where buckets were waiting to be emptied.

When the tank was full, Pa would drive to the sap house and connect the hose to the thirty-gallon tank. The sap would flow into the evaporator, which Pa had bought from his brother-in-law, Perl Thomas, a salesman for the important equipment.

Maple syrup, Pa's biggest cash crop, was sold in gallon tin cans to merchants and some private customers.Five gallons would be kept for family use and gifts. The first syrup of the season was the best. When trees started to bud, syrup was darker and would be used for cooking, making taffy or maple sugar. Emma loved maple sugar shaved over homemade cottage cheese.

Uncle Perl had gone from selling evaporators to selling automobiles, the new fangled horseless carriages. He worked part-time for the Reo dealership. In fact, he bought himself a Reo, the first line of cars R.E.Olds manufactured. His was one of the first automobiles in Oceana County. Since automobiles were in the experimental stage, new laws were enacted to prevent fires. A garage for an automobile must be a safe distance from a home. Therefore, Uncle Perl had a garage built down the hill from his house, and several rods east of the store. The structure was covered with sheets of tin for safety's sake.

When summer came, Gladys Waterman came again for a visit with her country cousins. It was cherry-picking time in July. While they were picking cherries, Gladys asked, "Uncle Charlie, is this limb big enough to hold me?"

"Oh, yes, that limb would hold two little women your size."

Up she climbed to the branch, and down she fell as the branch split from the trunk.

Chapter 11

Gladys's right arm was very badly broken. It was a compound fracture with the bone protruding into the ground.

Pa ran to the barn, calling over his shoulder, "I'll call the doctor!" Instantly Pa was flying out the driveway and down the road bareback on Pet at a gallop. (A neighbor told them later, "I saw Charlie Shepherdson riding down the road as if the devil was after 'im!"

Meantime, Ma tried to cleanse the wound with lots of water. Gladys was quite calm, considering the seriousness of the injury. Emma and Pearl could only stand and watch, feeling terrible about their cousin's accident and carrying water and clean white cloths for Ma whenever she needed them.

In a surprisingly short time Emma could see a cloud of dust.Pa and Pet reappeared, coming from Aunt Lucy and Uncle Perl's store, over a mile away at Tigris. That was the closest telephone, where he had gone to call Dr. Munger in Hart.

Before long an even bigger cloud of dust could be seen coming down the road. It was Dr. Munger, speeding with his horse and buggy.

When the doctor arrived, he gave terse commands. "Place the child on the dining table! Bring me a basin of water, soap, and a towel! Light a lamp!"

He soon administered chloroform to Gladys, and Emma was assigned to hold the lamp so the doctor could see to set the arm.Soon Emma said, "Ma, I feel sick!" Pa took the lamp from her and told her to go outside for fresh air. The combination of the anesthetic and the traumatic injury were more than she could take.

The fresh air felt good. She breathed deeply as she sat down on the front step. The black dots that had started to close in on her vision were clearing away. Sport came and licked her hand, helping to divert her thoughts. "Sport, you're a good dog," she crooned to him as she stroked his silky ears. Pearl joined her there, and asked, "Are you all right, Emma?"

"Yes, I'll be all right out here, but I would've fainted if I'd stayed in there any longer. How about you? Are you all right?" She put an arm around Pearl's shoulder.

"Yeth, I'm all right," Pearl said, "but I didn't like being in there either. I'm glad I got to go to thcool latht year." Pearl had been held back from going to school until she was seven because of speech problems.

Emma began to giggle. "Yes, Pearly, I'm glad, too.We'll both go back to school in September.I was just thinking about something funny. Remember that Ma told us that if we got something in our eye, we should ask someone to blow in our eye to get it out?"

"Yeth," Pearl replied.

"Do you remember when you got something in your eye, and you knelt down in front of Sport and said, 'Bo, Port, bo!' (Blow, Sport,blow!)? You thought the dog would blow in your eye."

"Well, Port wath my friend. I knew he would want to help me," Pearl reasoned.

"You're getting better, Pearl. You can talk much better than you could last year."

"I hope tho."

Sport had helped to divert their attention from the grim realities going on in the house. He now lay at their feet with an occasional twitch of ear or swish of tail to chase flies.

Eventually the doctor came out, mopping his brow. Pa followed him to his buggy and untied the reins, handing them to the doctor who had climbed into the buggy. Pa took out his wallet, paid the doctor and thanked him for coming so promptly. Dr. Munger nodded in acknowledgement, then clicked his tongue to his horse, and he was gone.

The girls found Gladys lying on the spindle sofa, asleep, with a cast on her arm. "Emma, will you please watch Gladys until she wakes up? Call me when she stirs," Ma said.

Gladys returned to her home in Hart in a few days. She made a fair recovery, though her arm remained a little stiff.

One day when Ma was at the store, Aunt Lucy said, "Bessie, could you ask Charlie to come and stay with Perl this afternoon? He's very sick. The doctor's been here, and he can't seem to do much for 'im. He says there's something wrong with Perl's kidneys." Her face was grave.

"Yes, of course, Lucy. I'll tell Charlie. He'll come right away. When did Perl take sick?"

"It started yesterday morning. He's been having these bad backaches, but he thought he'd strained his back lugging things for the store. Then yesterday morning the pain went from bad to worse. I'm real worried."

"Emma, put those groceries and cloth I bought in the basket and come. Hurry, we need to hustle home and call your pa," Ma ordered.

Standing nearby, Emma had heard the whole conversation, so she snatched the articles from the counter, dropping them into the basket, and followed her mother quickly to their single-seated canopy buggy. Ma gave Pet the reins, and he soon covered the distance to the Shepherdson farm.

Emma jumped out of the buggy and ran to the house to

tell Pa about Uncle Perl. Pa met her at the back door with the *GRAND RAPIDS PRESS* in his hand.

"What's all the hurry?"

"Uncle Perl's sick bad. Aunt Lucy wants you to go stay with him!" Emma cried.

Pa hurried to meet Ma, coming from the buggy. "It's his kidneys, Charlie. The Doctor says he can't do anything."

"I'll go and stay with him as long as he needs me, Bessie. Tell Lester to take care of the chores." He stored the buggy in the shed and mounted Pet, bareback and sped down the road.

"Pa stayed several days until Uncle Perl died.Aunt Lucy called the Reo dealership and asked for a suitable vehicle to come and take Uncle Perl's body to the undertaker. A vehicle was sent, and Aunt Lucy accompanied him to the funeral home and expressed his wish to be creamated. Both the moving of his body by motor vehicle and his cremation were unusual and widely discussed in the community, thought by some to be sacrilegious.

Pa and Ma attended Uncle Perl's memorial service, conducted by spiritualists, but their children did not.

The previous summer Lena had attended Ypsilanti State Teachers' College, but both she and Vina were home that summer. Vina and Roy Perry were engaged, with plans to be married in October. She was busy preparing her trousseau.

Lena hired a stone mason to replace the wooden front porch with a concrete and stone one. She had taught the previous year at Ferry. The lady with whom she boarded attended the Wesleyan Church and invited Lena to attend. During a revival meeting in the winter Lena received Jesus Christ as her Savior.

Lena had also met Will Leicht from the Brooks neighborhood, and he was coming that summer to court her. On one of Will's visits he called, "Emma, I have a present for you."

"Oh, Will, what is it?" Emma asked.

"It's a surprise. I have something that I don't use any more. I think you can make good use of it, so I've brought it to give to you." With this he brought out a beautiful saddle from the buggy and presented it to Emma.

"It's beautiful, Will! Thank you so much.I'll use it to go down the lane to get the cows for Pa. I don't ride bareback as well as he does." She threw her arms around Will's neck and gave him a big hug.

Will was a meat cutter in a grocery store in Hart. Sometimes when he came to visit Lena, he arrived on Saturday, stayed in the front room bedroom overnight, and returned to his home on Sunday night.

Lena returned to Ferry School in the fall, and Emma and Pearl returned to Sackrider School.

October soon came, and plans were in full swing for Vina and Roy's wedding.

Chapter 12

The wedding of the year was to be at Sackrider Church. Having never attended a church wedding, Emma waited with much anticipation. Lena made a screen to be decorated with autumn leaves.She continued the fall color theme for the whole front of the church.

Vina was lovely in a white wool dress, and the autumn leaves were a perfect backdrop for her beautiful auburn hair. Roy was a tall handsome groom dressed in a dark brown suit. The young Rev. George Shepherdson, home for a year from Central College in Huntington, Indiana, performed the ceremony for his sister and brother-in-law.

A striking pair they were as they left the church with horse and two-seated buggy, trailing tin cans and old shoes to the Shepherdson home! After a sumptuous chicken dinner, Vina and Roy loaded their luggage into the buggy with the fringed canopy. They disconnected all but the "Just Married" sign and set off with George for Hart.

They arrived in time for the train that would start them on their honeymoon. As a railroad employee, Roy had rail passes to take them to Denver, an unusually long wedding trip for a couple in rural Michigan in 1908.

Since Uncle Perl had died, Aunt Lucy invited Vina and

Roy to live with her and help in the store. That seemed an agreeable arrangement, so Roy left the railroad and became a storekeeper when they returned from Colorado.

A week after the couple's return to the community the young people of the neighborhood organized a belling, and on Saturday night they made their way quietly to Aunt Lucy's house. They hated to disturb her, but they couldn't miss the opportunity for a shivaree. They parked their buggies along the road and tied their horses to roadside trees, so they could approach the house silently on foot. They came prepared with all sorts of noisemakers: bells, old pans, and even a drum to beat.Stealthily the group circled the darkened house. Then the clangor began! Bells, pans, and drum were all attacked at once, making a terrible din until the bride and groom appeared at the door, tousled, but grinning.

Someone had brought a wheelborrow, and the crowd insisted that Vina get into it, and that Roy wheel her. The noisemakers followed down the driveway, accompanying the wonderful ride with their noise. Down to the store they went, then down the road to the tin garage, up that drive and around the square back to the house. Vina finished her ride good-naturedly, and Roy asked them all to wait while he went down to the store to find treats for them. He soon returned with long sticks of candy in assorted flavors.After he had handed them around, the "guests" left, satisfied, laughing, talking, and licking their sticks of candy, noisemakers silent.

With Vina away from home, Ma needed more help with cooking and baking.Emma became the apprentice in the kitchen, learning how to make many things, including bread and delicious fruit pies.

Rosa Perry, Emma and Pearl kept track of whose turn it was to have the newlyweds come for Sunday dinner, the Perrys or the Shepherdsons.

The school year went quickly. Emma enjoyed her school

work and her friends, though she sometimes wondered if she would ever have a beau and a beautiful wedding like Vina's. With her plain face and straight, light hair, would she attract a fine young man?

Sometimes older boys at school played practical jokes. One day a strange thing happened. Occasionally a bell sounded near the front of the room. No bell was in sight. The sound seemed to come from under the floor. The second time it sounded, Miss Cargill marched purposefully to the back of the room, down the basement steps and to the area under the platform. There under the floor was the offending bell with a wire attached to it, running toward the back of the room and through a knothole in the floor.

She quickly reappeared and studied the floor until she discovered a small wire loop sticking through that hole in the floor. It was under the desk of Charlie Hull. When he bumped the wire loop with his foot, the bell would tinkle near the front of the room. So Charlie was the culprit! Emma had not suspected him. She never did find out how or if he was punished. He might have been threatened with the loss of his job as janitor.

Charlie was a good friend of George and Lester.When they were at home, he often came to visit them, sleeping in the Shepherdson barn with them sometimes in the summer.

This was the year George had stayed home to help with the farm work, so Lester could take a business course at Central College in Huntington, Indiana.George made frequent visits to the Hull home. Sometimes he went to visit Charlie, and sometimes he went to visit the teacher, Miss Dema Cargill. She boarded with Hulls next door to the school, as teachers often did.

At school one day Lucile Hodges said, "Vina's pregnant, isn't she, Emma?"

"Pregnant?I don't know," Emma replied with surprise. Yes, indeed she discovered it was true. She was going to be an aunt. That would be wonderful! She could hardly wait for the arrival of the Vina's baby!

In March a Christian Endeavor part at the Shepherdsons' home ended with the making of delicious maple taffy. The lively teenagers scooped up plates full of clean snow and held them out for Mrs. Shepherdson or Emma to pour boiling maple syrup onto the snow.

With April came lots of rain, muddy roads and Pearl's birthday. At school on Emma's birthday she took her seat before the bell rang at the end of the lunch hour.

Before she knew what was happening, a boy sat down on each side of her and began kissing her on the cheek. One would kiss her right cheek; then the other would kiss her left for a total of fifteen kisses. Her cheeks were fiery red before they finished. The boys were Charlie Hull and Arthur Sills.They triumphantly took their own seats as the bell rang.

Emma's cheeks were still glowing amid a hearty ripple of laughter as the students all took their seats. She liked both boys equally well at that time. They gave her a birthday gift to remember.

There were no girls in Charlie Hull's family. He was the middle boy with older brother Jake twenty-six, and younger brother Lewie ten.Mrs. Nellie Hull bemoaned the fact that she had no girls to "pretty up the house" like Bessie Shepherdson did. She still grieved for her little girl Anabel, who had died when she was three, and she encouraged neighbor girls to come to visit her.

Chapter 13

As Emma rounded the corner into Hulls' driveway, her classmate Charlie was helping his mother into their canopy buggy. "I guess I came at a bad time," Emma said, making her presence known and flipping her long single braid over her shoulder.

"No such thing, Emma," Mrs. Hull said, catching her breath. "We were just going over to Hoffmyers' place for a visit. We won't be gone long. You hop right up here and go along with us."

"Sure thing," Charlie said. "Come on, Emma."

While Emma was wondering where she would sit in the buggy seat made for two, Charlie gave her a hand, and his mother said, "You sit right here on my lap." Taking Charlie's hand, Emma stepped up into the buggy, lowered herself onto Mrs. Hull's ample lap, and Charlie squeezed in beside them.

With a cluck from Charlie to the sleek bay horse, they were out of the drive, turning south and down the hill.

After a pleasant visit with the Hoffmyers, the three travelers started back. They were chatting comfortably when they saw a cloud of dust coming toward them. It was an automobile, a rare sight on the road in 1909 in rural Oceana County. As it came closer, Charlie was trying to decide if it was a Reo or a Ford when Prince decided he didn't care which it was. He didn't like it coming at him. He jerked the buggy first right, then left, and pawed the air with his forelegs. Emma was breathing quickly, and her heart was pounding. She felt so helpless. All she could do was pray silently, "Dear God, please help Charlie get the horse under control. Please protect us!"

"Down, Prince!" Charlie commanded. Then more quietly, "It's all right, Prince. Down,boy. Down boy. Attaboy, Prince. Good boy."

"Oh, I'm so relieved!" Emma cried."We could've been killed!"

"I might as well have been," Charlie said.It wouldn't have been much loss."

"Don't talk that way, Charlie." Emma was shocked.

"Those wretched, new-fangled cars!"Mrs. Hull said. There should be a law against them being on the same road with horses. They scare the poor things to death."

Two hours later as Emma was in her room getting ready for bed, she kept thinking about what Charlie had said. It disturbed her so much that she sat down at her study table to write him a note:

Thursday, June 10, 1909

Dear Charlie,

I was really upset about what you said this evening when we almost had an accident. After the automobile had passed us, and you had Prince under control, you said you might as well have been killed. That was a terrible thing to say, Charlie, especially since you aren't saved.You aren't ready to die!

Sincerely,

Emma

She folded the note and wrote Charlie's name on the

outside. She left it on her table and knelt beside her straw-mattress bed to pray.Before she closed her eyes, she traced the pattern of her patchwork quilt with her finger. Life was as complicated as her quilt pattern. Why would Charlie say what he did about dying? In the morning she would take the note down to the corner and put it into Charlie's mailbox.

The next evening as Emma was emptying the dishwater into the sink, Charlie knocked at the back door. "Why, Hello, Charlie, how are you today?" she greeted.

"I was thinking about what you said in your note as I was cutting peas to sell to the new Roach Canning Factory, so I came to talk to you about it," he said.

"Oh, I'm glad you did. Let me put this dishpan away and take off my apron. Then we can go sit in the lawn swing and talk."

The swing, made with a wooden frame and two double seats facing each other was a convenient place to talk. Charlie shared a seat with Emma. "What did you mean when you said I'm not saved?"

"Maybe I shouldn't have said that, but I've heard you swear in the school yard, and I didn't think you were saved," Emma said.

"Is swearing so bad?"

"It's taking the Lord's name in vain." Jesus shed his blood on the cross to forgive our sins. Why should we take His name in vain?"

"I never thought about it that way. What does it mean to be saved?"

"It's asking Jesus to forgive our sins and make us a child of God."

"Have you been saved?"Charlie asked.

"Yes, I was saved at church when I was eleven."

"What was it like?What did you do?"

"I went forward at church, knelt at the altar, and prayed to Jesus to forgive my sins. I knew I had sinned, but that

Jesus loved me and shed His blood so I could be forgiven and have peace in my heart."

"How do you pray? Do you just talk like we're talking, or do you have to kneel kown?"

"It's like talking to another person, and when we kneel to pray, it's just for respect and reverence for God. You can pray walking down the road or doing anything.Sometimes I pray while I wash dishes."

"Do you really?"

"Sure, it's as natural as breathing."

"You've given me a lot to think about. I'd better be going now, but suppose I have some more questions. Can I come again and talk to you?"

"Of course. You can come anytime to talk," Emma said.

"Then I'll probably come tomorrow night after I finish my chores."

"Fine, I'll see you tomorrow." Her heart was lighter as she walked to the house, stooping long enough to pick a cluster of purple English violets. She loved their rich color and delicate shape. They were iridescent in the sun. At least Charlie was willing to talk, and he'd be coming again. The Lord was answering her prayers.

He did come the next day and the next and the next.

One evening her brother George drove the two-seated canopy buggy and took Charlie and Emma to their teacher, Dema Cargill's home several miles away for the evening. Another time George and Dema, Charlie and Emma went to town in the buggy, with the older couple taking the back seat, leaving Charlie to drive.George hung a curtain between the seats to give a little more privacy. There were other times when the two couples shared the lawn swing to talk.

On Sunday, July 4, 1909, Charlie went forward to receive Christ as his Savior at the close of the morning worship service. He was wearing a happy smile as he shook hands with Emma, "Now I know what you mean by peace," he said.

"I'm so happy for you," she said, beaming. Further conversation would have to wait. Other people were anxious to shake hands with Charlie, too.

The next evening as they sat in the lawn swing, Emma said, "Thank God for answering my prayers for you!"

"Thank you for praying for me, and for being willing to talk to me about it. You helped me a good deal."

Emma's oldest sister Lena noticed Charlie's visits, and she took Emma aside. "Emma, how would you like to have a gold watch and chain?"

"Why, of course I'd love to have one, but why do you ask?"

"Because I'll give you a watch and chain if you don't have a beau until you're eighteen."

"Oh, Lena, Charlie's just been saved, and he needs my help and encouragement.I can't desert him now."

"Well, you're very young to have a serious relationship. You'd better think about it."

Chapter 14

Tears were streaming down Emma's face when she flung herself across her bed. She knew that a gold watch and chain were very expensive and very beautiful. What girl wouldn't want one? She thought about Aunt Lucy's beautifully engraved one that looked so pretty on her good black dress.

Then she thought of Charlie, dear Charlie.How could she possibly break off her relationship with him now when he needed her?He might think she had only been interested in his becoming a Christian. She was interested in his spiritual welfare, but she also cared about him as a friend, a dear friend, who now needed her help and encouragement in his new faith.

Emma's mind was made up. She washed her face with cold water. She would tell Lena her decision. It was very generous of Lena to offer a beautiful watch, but Charlie was more important than any gold watch.

All attention was soon turned to Vina.Preparations for her baby were interrupted by early labor.Roy called Dr. Munger and sent for Jenny Neusdoffer to come and assist Vina. Aunt Lucy made her as comfortable as possible in her own downstairs bedroom. The doctor and midwife had plenty of time to come. Vina was in labor many hours and had a difficult delivery, but a tiny baby Dorothy arrived on July 9. Dr. Munger pointed out to Vina and Jenny the immature fingernails of the premature baby.

Dorothy was the first grandchild on both sides of her family, so she brought special joy to both the Perrys and the Shepherdsons. Lester saw the baby before Emma did, so she asked him, "What does she look like, or who does she look like?"

"She's red," was his reply.

After Vina had had a few weeks to recover, the Sunday visits became even more precious than before. Rosa, Emma, and Pearl looked forward even more keenly to them with the living doll to hold.

An important work event of the summer was threshing day. It was strenuous, but a time of pleasureable teamwork. Individual farm families did the preliminary work. First they cut the grain with a binder, which also tied the grain into bundles and dropped them. After this process, the bundles were made into small stacks in the field, so they would dry.

On threshing day bundles were loaded onto wagons and fed into the threshing machine. The grain came out one spout into a bag. Straw was blown out a taller spout, forming a straw stack. Men had to tie up the bags of grain and load them onto a wagon from which they would be moved for storage. It was hot, dusty work, but all the men of the community who had raised wheat worked together to thresh it. They followed the threshing machine from farm to farm, until all the grain that was ripe was harvested. When fields of oats or another grain were ripe, the process was repeated.

Emma and Pearl were amused at Uncle Silas wearing his shirttail outside his trousers. It was unusual, but it probably kept chaff from getting into his pants.

While the men were sweating at their labor, the women were standing over a hot cook stove. Emma and Pearl helped Ma and Lena prepare a meal for the crew of men. On this threshing day they cooked a delicious roast beef dinner with berry pies for dessert. On the back porch Emma placed a wash basin, a pail of warm water, bar of soap, and a towel for the men to use.

The table was extended and spread with an abundance of food. Threshers had notorious appetites. "Silas, will you please ask the blessing on the food?" Pa asked after the men had gathered around the table. The men really enjoyed their food.Emma and Pearl were busy carrying empty dishes to the kitchen to be loaded with more food and refilling glasses with water or lemonade.

After the kitchen was cleaned up, Emma watched the men at work. She heard Pat Perysian say, "That's the bag I've been looking for." She looked at it curiously, but she couldn't see that it was different from all the others.The difference was that it was the last one to be filled. The men enjoyed the joke.

The next series of events seemed to happen like Dominoes going down. The first thing that happened was that Grandma Ridge died very suddenly.

After her funeral Grandpa sold his house and little farm to Roy and Vina. They moved from Aunt Lucy's house to the new little one with baby Dorothy.

Emma made plans to rent a room upstairs in Grandpa's new home on Dryden Street in Hart to attend high school.

She invited Rose Foster to share the room with her.Rose was a sister of the boy Bess Waterman was seeing. They both looked at the room and planned what they would need to bring from home. Grandpa provided them with a three-burner kerosene stove for their cooking.

On Charlie Hull's next visit he announced, "Father has arranged with his brother, Uncle Israel, for me to stay with him, work on his farm near Shelby, and attend Shelby High School."

"Oh, Charlie, you won't be going to Hart High School

with the rest of us? Emma asked, disappointed.

"No, I won't, but I'll probably be home some weekends, so I'll see you then, and we can compare notes on high schools, and we can write."

"Yes," she said, "of course. It's not so far away. It's only six miles from Hart, but it's that much farther from home."

"I expect to work for my board and ride my wheel (bicycle) from the farm. It's only about a mile and a half to school, so it won't be so bad," he said taking her hand. "But I'll miss our evening talks."

"I will too, but we'll both be busy with our school work."

"I'll miss you though, Emma," and he squeezed her hand.

"Hurrah!" came the call from Pa from the front door. That was his signal for curfew.

Charlie gave her a light kiss on the cheek, and he was off on his bicycle, heading home.

"Shelby!" she said to herself as she went inside. "That's too far away."

Chapter 15

While Emma packed a trunk to move to her new boarding place at Grandpa Ridge's house, she had mixed feelings. She was excited about the adventure. She loved school. Some of her friends would be there, but not Charlie, and many of her classmates would be strangers. She didn't know Rose Foster very well. She seemed very nice, but would they get along well, sharing the same space, cooking together?

Ma gave Emma a few dishes and cooking utensils to pack in a trunk. She packed towels and washcloths between the dishes to protect them on the trip by wagon into town.

As she packed, her mind kept going to Charlie. She hated the idea of his going to Shelby High School instead of Hart. She would miss their frequent talks, but he said he would be home some weekends, and, of course, they could write. Maybe it wouldn't be so bad.

Sunday, September 5, 1909, was a very special day. Both Emma and Charlie were baptized in Huftile Creek in an afternoon service, by their tall presiding Elder, Rev. J.S. Beers, who had come to conduct Quarterly Meeting on Saturday and Sunday.

After the baptismal service she waved goodbye to Charlie, as he rode his bicycle toward Shelby.Back home

Lester helped her load her luggage into the wagon. He had come home early in the summer from Central College in Huntington, Indiana, where he had gone to take a commercial course, and he was also on the basketball team. George had already returned by train to Huntington to resume his theological studies. They would all miss him. In fact, when George was ready to leave, Lester disappeared into the woods. It was too hard to tell his brother goodbye.

When Lester and Emma had everything loaded, she gave Ma a kiss and Pearl a hug. "Don't worry, Emma, even if someone snubs you as a country girl," Lester said as he helped Emma up to her seat on the wagon. Pa took the seat beside her, clucked to the horses, and they were off for a new chapter in her life.

When they arrived, dust-covered, at Grandpa's house on Dryden Street in Hart, Pa helped her carry the trunk. They followed Grandpa into the house to the stairway. Before they reached the top step the trunk had become very heavy and awkward to handle. "I'm glad you put handles on both ends of this trunk, Pa," Emma said, puffing.

"You must have brought all your mother's dishes," he said tugging on the heavy trunk.

"Not quite," Emma said laughing.

Pa went downstairs to visit with his father-in-law while she carried everything else upstairs. She dropped into a chair to rest for a minute and wipe the perspiration. It was September, but the days were still quite warm. Emma allowed herself only a minute before jumping up and arranging the room. One corner would be their kitchen.

Rose soon arrived with her own supply of dishes and food. "Oh, Rose, I know we're going to have a good time this year!"

"I'm sure we will. Look, I've brought sweet corn, tomatoes, and green beans."

"Wonderful!And I brought potatoes, some canned beef,

and a black raspberry pie."

"We'll have a feast," Rose said. "I brought some oatmeal for our breakfast and chocolate cake."

"Do you think two loaves of bread will last us for a week?"

"I should think so. I'll bring bread next week."

"That's fine," Emma said. "I'll go down and fill this pail with water so we can start cooking."

"I'll go with you and fill the pitcher, so we can wash our hands.I see your grandpa has put a 'thunder mug' under the bed for us to use at night."

"Yes, and there's an outhouse in the backyard."

"Emma, what do you want to be when you get out of school?" Rose asked as they followed the outdoor path to the pump for water.

"A teacher. How about you?"

"I've always wanted to be a nun since I was just a little girl. I might also be a teacher."

"I don't know much about nuns. Can they be teachers too?"

"Oh, yes, lots of nuns are teachers," Rose replied.

They pumped water for each other and soon filled both the pail and the pitcher and carried them upstairs. Are you nervous about tomorrow?" Rose asked.

"Yes, although I've had what was supposed to be two years of high school at Sackrider."

"Really?How did that happen? I thought your school only went through eighth grade like ours."

So Emma told her the story of the second room and second teacher at Sackrider School.

"Is that so? Hm, then if you had two years there, are you ready to start eleventh grade classes?"

"No, I wish I could, but we didn't earn that many credits in the two years. In fact, I haven't even enough credits to be a sophomore, but I'll take sophomore classes. I'll have to catch up somewhere along the way."

After eating a very tasty supper and organizing their room, they prepared for bed. Emma knelt on one side of the bed with her Bible open, read a passage, and bowed her head and prayed. With her rosary and prayer book, Rose knelt on the other side of the bed and had her devotions.

In the morning Rose cooked breakfast while Emma carried the chamber pot out and emptied it in the outhouse, rinsed it, and also carried a pail of fresh water up to their room. They fluffed the straw mattress and made their bed.

Emma was thinking, "I believe we can work together. I think Rose'll be a good roommate."

They took turns using the big china bowl to wash up. Rose brushed her beautiful dark hair and braided it into two braids. Emma braided hers into one thick braid down her back.

The girls walked the few blocks to school and joined the other students in the assembly hall. They were given their schedules and told where to sit with their own classes. Emma soon saw Lucile and Frank from Sackrider. That made her feel a little better.

The assembly was led by the principal,Mr. Arehart.After his short speech, he made some announcements. "Remember where your seat is here in the Assembly Hall. That will be your home base through the school year. Store your books there and return to it for your study hall periods, at noon and at the end of the day before you march out together."

Emma's first class was algebra. That class shouldn't be too difficult. They were given their books and an assignment for the next day with some time to study before they changed classes.

"We'll be reading 'The Legend of Sleepy Hollow' for tomorrow," her English teacher announced.

The next period was study hall, so she returned to the Assembly Hall and finished her math assignment. After third hour she stayed in her seat until the other students returned.

The study hall teacher announced, "All rise!March!" The first row marched out, then the other rows in order. When it was her turn, Emma marched in step down the hall, out the front entrance, down the many steps and the walk to the public sidewalk. She joined Rose there, and they hurried home for lunch.

World history was next.Ugh! She hated history. Botany and another study hall were followed by the formal exit march.

Before Emma knew it Friday had arrived, and Lester came with the buggy to take her home for the weekend. What about Charlie? Would he ride all the way home from Shelby to Hart and then to Sackrider on his bicycle? Would he be there before she was? Would he come to see her tonight, or wouldn't he be home until Saturday or not at all?

Chapter 16

"My old friend, Pet!" she greeted the horse with caresses after exchanging hugs with Lester. You're the most beautiful horse in the world, and I'm so glad to see you."

On the way home in the buggy Lester asked, "Well, how did you like Hart High School, Em?"

" I liked it.The teachers are nice, and so far I'm able to handle the assignments. History's not my favorite, but I think I'll be able to do the work."

"How about your roommate? Do you think you'll be able to get along together for the year?'

"Oh, yes, Rose Foster is a dear.I think we'll get along just fine. On Wednesday night I went to prayer meeting at the Congregational Church. Of course Rose didn't go with me because she's Catholic, but we get along very well. She's always cheerful; she does her share of work; and she brought delicious food from home, lots of vegetables and a chocolate cake.

"What's been happening at home? How's Pearly, and Baby Dorothy?" Emma asked.

"Pearly's fine. We all miss you. Dorothy was smiling when I saw her yesterday."

"It seems like I've been away at least a month. I can

hardly wait to see everyone!"

"That's understandable, because you've started a whole new pattern for your life, and you're making new friends. With all your new experiences you almost seem to be seeing through different eyes."

"Yes, Lester, you do understand, don't you?"

"Yes, of course I do. I had the same experience when I went to Huntington last year."

"Come on, Pet, you can make it up Damrell Hill. It's a long hard climb, but you can make it," Lester encouraged after they'd crossed Huftile Creek. "Ma asked me to stop on the way home and buy some things at Aunt Lucy's store."

They rode in silence for a few minutes. "There's Aunt Lucy's place!" she cried. "Isn't it a pretty setting up on that hill, with the barn behind and the store down by the road? The willow trees and maples on the road bank almost hide the house."

"Yes, and I love the view of the valley across the road and the hills in the distance." He pulled up to a hitching rail in front of the store and tied the reins.

Emma gave Aunt Lucy a hug as they entered the store. "Well, how's our Hart High School girl?" Aunt Lucy asked.

"I'm just fine, Aunt Lucy. May I look at your material while Lester buys some things? I need something new for winter."

"Of course.Look to your heart's content," and Aunt Lucy turned her attention to Lester.

Emma looked at the heavier fabrics. A dark green serge caught her attention .She would use last year's best dress for school this year, so she needed a new winter dress for Sunday. She'd talk to Ma and Lena about it. Lena was so good to help with her sewing. She embroidered beautiful designs on some of the dresses.

Lester soon finished the grocery shopping, and they were on their way home. Home had never seemed so precious.

Sport came first, barking his greeting and turning in circles in his eagerness to see her. Then Pearl came running out to meet her and exchange hugs. "Emma I missed you so," she greeted.

"I missed you too, Pearly. You'll have to come in and see my new room and meet my roommate."

"I'd like that," Pearl replied.

Emma was soon in Ma's arms. "How did you get along your first week?" Ma asked.

"Just fine, Ma, but I brought a list of things I need I won't need to take bread this week, because Rose is bring bread this time."

"That's good. Maybe you can just alternate weeks for bread. You can take other things, beets and carrots and bacon besides what you want to bake, maybe some cookies this time. How about some bread pudding?"

"That sounds good, Ma.Is Lena coming home for the weekend?"

"Yes, but Lester'll go to Ferry for her tomorrow morning."

Emma helped Ma with the supper, and she rushed to greet Pa when he came in from the barn.

"How goes it, Em?" he greeted.

"Fine, Pa. I like school, and I like Rose."

"That's good to hear, Em. Now will you ask the blessing on the food?"

"Sure, Pa.Thank you, Lord, for a good first week of school, and thank you for my beautiful family. Thanks too for the food.In Jesus'name, Amen."

After the supper dishes were done, Emma looked at *THE CHRISTIAN CONSERVATOR* (The United Brethren monthly) hanging on a sharp hook on the living room wall, next to *THE MICHIGAN CHRISTIAN ADVOCATE* (the Methodist publication). She scanned the new paper before playing a game of Dominoes, with Lester, Pa, and Pearl.Lester won that game.Next they played a game of

Authors.Emma won that one. Competition was keen, and they all enjoyed the games.

Next morning before breakfast Ma started yeast with sugar and warm water to make bread. By the time the family had enjoyed breakfast and Morning Worship, the yeast was foamy and ready for the rest of the ingredients.

While Ma made bread, Emma made sugar cookies from Ma's recipe, with a raisin in the middle of each one. Fresh rolls and cookies were both on the menu for dinner, giving a very inviting aroma when Lester arrived with Lena for the weekend.

As they were washing dishes, Emma talked to Ma and Lena about a new winter dress. Ma would not promise, but said, "I'll see about that." They might buy the green serge in a week or two.Lena said she'd be happy to help with it. She told them that Will would be coming that evening to see her, and that he would be staying overnight. She might need help getting the spare bedroom ready for him.Emma promised her help.

When the evening meal was finished and the dishes washed, Charlie appeared on his bicycle. "Good evening, Mr. Shepherdson," he greeted Pa in the yard as he parked his wheel and tipped his cap.

"I understand you're going to Shelby High School."

"Yes, sir, and I'm working for my board on my Uncle Israel's farm near there."

"What does he raise?" Pa asked.

"He has corn and potatoes and different kinds of fruit trees—apples, peaches, plums, and cherries."

"Is that so?And did you ride your wheel all the way from Shelby?"

"Yes, sir, I did. I had a flat tire too. I was near Hart, so I had to walk in and buy a repair kit and fix it before I could come on home. There's enough material in the kit to fix another flat, so I'll carry it with me."

"That sounds like a good idea," Pa replied, walking toward the house. "Here comes Emma."

Emma's eyes sparkled as she came out to see Charlie. They shook hands and walked to the swing in the front yard. "How was your week, Emma?"

"It was fine," and she told him all about it. "And how was yours?"

"It was all right, but I have a different feeling about my subjects. History will be my favorite.I find it very interesting. Math is fine too, but the English class may be a little more difficult. If you remember, I never did so well in those spell-downs we used to have, as you did."

"To each his own. How about the farm work and boarding with your aunt and uncle?"

"So far, it's all right." I help Uncle Izzy with the harvesting: digging potatoes, cutting corn, picking peaches and plums. I'll help with work in the fields and the orchards, depending on the season. Aunt Loey is a very good cook, and it's not far to ride my wheel into Shelby to school, just a mile and a half, so it's not bad at all. The worst part about it is that I can't see you every day," and he took her hand.

"I miss you too," and she gave his hand a squeeze, "but that'll make the weekends all the more special."

They talked of their friends.Some were going on to high school, and others had decided, for various reasons, not to continue their education. Adult responsibilities had already come for them. Emma and Charlie agreed that they were among the fortunate ones to be able to go on to school.

Will Leicht arrived in a cloud of dust with his horse and buggy. He greeted the couple in the swing and stepped up on the front porch. Lena met him at the door, and they joined hands. Soon they both came out. He helped her into the buggy, untied the horse, and they were gone, almost before the dust had settled from his arrival.

All too soon came Pa's "Hurrah!" for the couple in the

swing. Charlie kissed Emma on the cheek, and they walked hand in hand to his bicycle. With a kiss on the other cheek, he was off, leaving both of Emma's cheeks glowing and her eyes bright as she entered the house, remembering that she needed to check on the readiness of the spare bedroom for Will.

Chapter 17

Emma woke with a start.She could hear a horse and buggy in the driveway. Who could it be? Oh, yes, it was probably Lena and Will.Emma had just gone to sleep, and now her heart was pounding, and it would take a while to settle down to sleep again. Lena and Will seemed to be getting quite serious. He was a fine man.Emma wondered if they would get married. Emma and Pearl really enjoyed the saddle he'd given them.

How about herself? Would she get married, or would she teach like her sisters for a few years first? Would it be Charlie or someone else, or no one at all? At this time she couldn't think of anyone else but Charlie, but who knew? Maybe that would change.

She soon heard Lena coming upstairs to go to her room, trying to be quiet.She might as well not bother. The horse and buggy were like an alarm.

Emma lay there thinking about the fact that Lena was a Christian now too. On weekends when she came home, she joined the rest of the family at church, and she was an even sweeter sister than before.

Then Emma thought of Charlie, how he had changed since becoming a Christian! No more swearing, and he seemed more cheerful. He seemed to have a new purpose in life. What a wonderful person he had become! She'd see him at church in the morning.

He was in her Sunday School class. He sat beside her and shared his Bible with her for the lesson. She felt a thrill each time his hand touched hers.

After church he walked home with her before returning to his home. He held her hands as they stood by the road talking. "Im going to miss Christian Endeavor on Sunday nights. I really enjoy it, and learn a lot, too. It's good experience, preparing a lesson, getting up and leading a meeting."

"I'll miss it too, but sometimes we may be able to get in on the C.E. parties if they have them Saturday night, maybe even on Friday night," Emma replied.

"But I miss you most of all, Emma. Be good to yourself, and have a good week." He squeezed her hands and kissed her nose as he turned to go. They'd both have to leave in the afternoon. He'd ride his bicycle to Shelby, and Lester would take her to Grandpa Ridge's house in Hart to be ready for school the next day.

Rose arrived at their room on Dryden Street soon after Emma did. The girls exchanged hugs and showed each other what they'd brought to share for the week. They got along very well, but Emma regretted one incident that happened that year. She'd brought mincemeat pie for them to share, and after they'd eaten the last two pieces on Friday, Emma happened to think that it was Friday and reminded Rose that there was meat in the pie.

Rose put her hands to her face. "Oh, I never thought about the meat in the pie! I'll have to confess it."

"Please forgive me, Rose. I shouldn't have drawn that to your attention."

"It's all right, Emma.I should have thought of it myself."

Pearl sometimes accompanied Pa or Lester when they drove into town to pick up Emma on Friday after school.

She was with Lester in the spring when he drove the team of work horses and wagon into town to help Emma move home for the summer. The heavy trunk of dishes, and all the other things that had accumulated during the year must be taken home. Many trips down the stairs with heavy loads for Lester and Emma and lighter ones for Pearl finally cleared Emma's things. She took Grandpa a small sack with three sugar cookies. She handed it to him as he stood, filling the doorway with his massive frame. He said, "Thank you, Darlin.' "And they said their "Good-byes."

Rose's father came, and the two good friends, Emma and Rose, hugged and promised to see each other in the fall. She and her father were repeating the loading process when Emma, Pearl, and Lester waved "Goodbye" and started away.

"Lena's gone to Huntington to visit George. She's supposed to be back today. We'll go to the train station and see," Lester said as he drove away from Grandpa's house.

"That's right, she got out of school last week.I wish I could have gone with her.I'd like to see Central College. Maybe I'll go there to college to learn how to be a teacher after I graduate from high school."

"The train's just pulling out. We're right on time," Lester said, not listening."There's Lena!"

"Hello, Lena," Emma greeted. "How's George?"

"Oh, he's fine. He's got a girlfriend named Nina."

"Nina Steman?" Lester asked.

"Yes, that's her name. Do you know her?" Lena asked.

"Not very well, but I've met her," he replied.

"What does she look like?" Emma asked.

"She's plump," Lester said.

"And she has pretty dark hair and brown eyes," Lena added."She seems like a lovely girl. George seems to think a lot of her."

"I wonder if he'll be the next one married," Emma commented.

"I wouldn't be surprised," Lena replied with a smile. She handed Lester her luggage to put on the wagon, then accepted his hand to help her up. "And how's Pearly?"

"I'm fine, Lena," and she gave her big sister a hug.

Saturday evening Will came to see Lena. Sunday morning Emma saw him come out of the spare bedroom off the parlor as usual. Then a few minutes later she saw Lena come out of the same bedroom in her nightgown. What was going on here?!

Chapter 18

"Lena, where did you sleep last night?" Emma asked, shocked.

"In the front room bedroom."

"And where did Will sleep?"

"In the front room bedroom," Lena replied to the inquisition. "We got married in Illinois." She left the room and came back, holding out her marriage certificate.

"You mean you eloped? Why in Illinois?"

"It's a long story. I got on the train in Hart. Will and his sister Augusta got on the train in Shelby, and we went to Huntington to have George marry us. Then we found out we'd have to wait too long to get the license, so we went to Illinois, where it doesn't take as long. We were married in Lincoln Park in Chicago."

"Why didn't you get married here, so we could all enjoy it? Why did you elope?" the curious Emma continued.

"We stayed overnight in Chicago, and then we came back on the train. Will and Gusty got off the train in Shelby, and as you know, I got off the train in Hart. We want to keep it a secret, so please don't tell people we're married," Lena explained.

"I think that's crazy, but I'll try to keep your secret outside the family," Emma agreed reluctantly. "Do Lester and Pearl know you're married? They didn't say anything about it."

"Probably not. No one knew until Will came yesterday. We told Ma and Pa last night."

"Well, I never!" Emma exclaimed."Lester," she said to her brother coming in from the barn, "did you know that Lena and Will are married? They eloped in Chicago."

"They eloped?!" he cried.

"Yes, they did," Emma replied and told him the story.

"Well, I'll be a monkey's uncle! Hello, Brother," he greeted Will, who was coming in from outdoors. "Is it true that you're now part of the family?"

"Yes, it is true," Will agreed and shook hands with Lester.

"Well, congratulations!" Lester said, pumping his hand. "Where did this wedding take place anyway?"

"Wedding? Whose wedding?" Pearl asked, coming into the room.

"Our wedding," Will admitted, smiling broadly. He was explaining the details when Lena came out of their room, brushing her beautiful long hair.

Lester grabbed her hair brush and paddled her playfully with it, before giving her a hug and wishing her a happy marriage.

They did all eventually get to church that morning, but Emma kept a tight seal on her lips. She didn't even tell Charlie the big secret, much as she wanted to.

Will Leicht was building a house in the Brooks neighborhood, but it was not finished, so Lena continued to live with her parents, and Will spent weekends with her.

In the next few days several people asked Emma, "Lena's married, isn't she?"

Emma would blush and try to give an evasive answer. She decided she was hiding very little. She probably might as well say, "Yes, she is," but she didn't. She decided at that time, "When I get married, everyone will know it. "Im not going to put people through that sort of embarrassment."

Charlie came often to see Emma during the summer, depending on the work he was doing. There were many evenings in the lawn swing and sometimes walks in the woods.

One evening in late August as they were sitting in the swing, Emma asked, "Charlie, are you going to go to Shelby High School again this year?"

"No, Emma, dear, I'm going to Hart High School this year, and we're in the process of finding me a boarding place. There's a lady my parents know that we're going to see about it. I'll let you know when I find out," he replied with some excitement in his voice.

"Oh, Charlie, I'm so glad.I hope you won't be far from where I'll be staying.Margaret Andrews and I've made arrangements to room in the upstairs of a Mrs. Laramy's house on State Street.Rose and I'll always be friends, but she's rooming with someone else this year."

As they were talking, Charlie's arm had reached around her shoulders." I'm really looking forward to it, Emma."

"Hurrah!" came Pa's curfew call.

They walked to the front door with his arm around her. Then he held her and kissed her on the lips before he dashed off on his bicycle.

Emma's heart was singing as she flew up the steps and into the house. "Ma, Charlie's going to Hart instead of Shelby to school this year. Isn't that great?"

"I don't know if it is or not. This is moving along pretty fast for a schoolgirl. You do want to graduate from high school, don't you?"

"Yes, of course, Ma. Don't worry. Goodnight,everybody."

"Goodnight, Emma," her parents and Lena said.

"Nice boy, Charlie," she heard her father say as she was preparing for bed.

A week later on one of Charlie's visits he said, "I have news, Emma.Mrs. Garwood has consented to have me as a boarder. She lives a few blocks from where you and Margaret will be staying, so I should be able to see you once in a while."

"Oh, Charlie, that's wonderful. You know I'll be taking physics this year, and I don't know anything about it, except that it'll be a hard subject. Maybe you can help me with it. You understand much more than I do about engines and things like that, and I'll be taking American history, too. Ugh, I know you can help me with that."

"And you can help me with spelling and literature," he added."It'll be wonderful to be able to see you every day at least at school," and he gave her a squeeze.

From left: Pearl Shepherdson (Peacock), Lena & Will Leicht, Lester, Emma, George, Roy & Vina Perry & Baby Dorothy. Center: Bessie & Charles Shepherdson

Chapter 19

"Charlie, are you ready to move into Hart?" Emma asked when he arrived one September evening.

"No, I won't be moving in for a while. I'll be riding my wheel into town every day for a few weeks."

"Oh, really, I thought you'd be moving in now," Emma was disappointed.

"Instead of packing my budget (bag), I was ordering Sunday School literature today for the last quarter."

"Oh, is that part of your job as Sunday School Secretary?" Emma asked.

"You bet," he replied."I have to keep track of how many lesson books, or picture cards, or Sunday School papers are needed in each class and order the right amount from church headquarters in Huntington in time for them to be here for the beginning of the next quarter."

"You haven't told me yet about your trip to Annual Conference. You were lay delegate from our circuit, weren't you?" Emma asked.

"Yes, I was. First I went by train to Eaton Rapids to see my cousins that I visited at Christmas.I was with them from Thursday until Monday, when I met your brother George at the train station in Lansing. He came up from Huntington for

Conference before coming on home for a visit. We went by train to Saginaw and then to Caro for Annual Conference. Your cousin Harry Harwood and I helped put up the tent for the meetings, and I was appointed to the Ways and Means Committee.

"There were many good messages, good meals, and good fellowship. Monday we took the train back to Lansing and stayed with one of my cousins. On Tuesday before train time we visited the botanical gardens at Michigan Agricultural College in East Lansing."

"It sounds like you enjoyed yourself."

"Yes, I did, very much so."

"And is it true that Jessie Harwood was appointed to be our new pastor?"

"Yes, it is true. By this time I suppose they're moving into the parsonage in Hart."

"We have a very interesting situation in our family this year. Lena is teaching at Sackrider school, and Pearl will be one of her scholars."

"And does everyone know by this time that Lena is Mrs. Leicht?" he asked.

"Oh, yes, when she got the job at the school, she had to tell the board that she was married."

Pa called curfew earlier that night because of the plan for the next day. Charlie held Emma close and kissed her good-night. How could she go to sleep early with such anticipation?

The following day after Sunday dinner, Lester hitched the horses to the wagon.Emma had been packing dishes, pots and pans, linens and clothing for days. She took one end of the heavy trunk and Lester took the other.Soon the wagon was loaded.

Margaret arrived shortly after Emma, and Mrs. Laramy showed them through the living room and up the stairs to the apartment where they would be staying. When they had everything upstairs, they both sat down to catch their breath and plan how to arrange the rooms. The spacious apartment was in order before each went to her own bed.

In the morning they met their friends Gracie Baker and her brother Harry as they were approaching the school. "Good morning, Gracie, did you get moved in? Where are you staying?" Emma asked.

"We're staying at Mrs. Gill's house. Yes, we moved in yesterday. Did you?"

"Yes, and here comes Charlie," Emma replied, her face lighting up.

He was smiling too as he saw her among their friends. He parked his bicycle and wiped perspiration from his forehead before joining them. "Well, good morning, Everyone!" He stopped to catch his breath. "It's good to be among friends. Last year at Shelby everyone was a stranger. They were friendly though. I soon got acquainted with some of them."

"I think we'd better go in," Emma prompted, and they all started moving up the steps of their beautiful brick and stone school building. Charlie's hand touched Emma's momentarily on the handrail as they climbed the steps.

By the first of October they had settled into a sort of routine. Charlie had moved into Hart, and at least one night a week he came to Emma and Margaret's apartment, ostensibly to help Emma with physics or history. On Thursday nights when he came by, they joined him in attending prayer meeting. Occasionally Emma and Margaret went to his room to visit or ask for help.

One crisp fall day after school Charlie came to the girls' apartment and said, "Emma, I'm going over to see the Harwoods. Do you want to go along?"

"Yes, I think I can. Sure, just let me tidy up my hair."

They walked hand-in-hand along several blocks to the parsonage next to the little red brick church that was also on the circuit with Sackrider Church.

Sadie answered their knock. "Why, hello, Emma and

Charlie, how's school going?"

"Fine, first rate," Charlie replied.

"Fine, with Charlie's help, Emma added.

Sadie laughed, and Jessie came in from his study. He gave his cousin Emma a hug and Charlie a hand. "Have a chair and make yourselves comfortable," he greeted, sitting near them. Sadie soon reappeared with their two little girls Anna and Ruth, who had warm greetings for Emma and shy ones for Charlie.

"Charlie, would you consider being nominated for Sunday School superintendent in December?" Jessie asked.

"Don't you think I'm pretty young for that kind of responsibility?" Charlie asked.

"No, you've taken the position of Sunday School Secretary seriously, and I think you could handle the job of superintendent. Would you be willing to be nominated?"

"Why, yes, I suppose I'd be willing to be nominated if you think I can do it. That's not saying I'll be elected."

"I'm sure you could do it," Jessie said. "We need young blood and young ideas. All right, with your permission I'll recommend your name for nomination in the Sunday School election coming up in December. How are you doing with your German studies, Emma?"

"It's very interesting and challenging. I'm practicing a few phrases to try on Will Leicht. He speaks German, you know."

"Yes, I know. That should be a challenge. He'll know the proper accent. Charlie, are you playing football this year?" Jessie asked.

"Yes, I am. We practice on the fairground."

"How have your games been going?"

"We beat Shelby two weeks ago, and last Friday night we beat Whitehall 12-6."

"Sounds like you're doing very well," Jessie commented. "What's this I hear about you singing in an Oratorio?"

"Yes, in December we'll be presenting the *Oratorio Ruth*. We did it last year in Shelby, and we're doing it this year in Hart. I'm also involved in the Rhetoric Junior Club and helped to organize the Lyceum, so I'm very busy."

"I should say you are! What subjects are you enjoying this year?"

"I spend a lot of time with chemistry.It's very interesting; I enjoy the lab work, and of course, I like history. I think we'd better be heading back, Emma. We'll see you on Sunday." He helped Emma with her coat. Then he put on his own jacket and flat, wool cap.They said goodbyes and left.

Charlie found it difficult to be asked to be a pallbearer for the funeral of their school friend Stella Carr. He did as he was asked, and many of their school friends attended the funeral.It made him think seriously about life, plans, death.

The following day he stopped by Emma's apartment and asked her to go for a walk with him. After putting on her coat, she joined him. They walked several blocks east to a wooded ravine. He took her hand and led her down a path leading to the bottom of the ravine. There they found a log where they could sit and talk. After the normal chit-chat, Charlie said, putting his arm around her, "Emma, I don't know where the Lord is going to lead me in life, but I hope you won't be far away."

His lips found hers, and they held each other close for some minutes, when they relaxed and continued their conversation.

Frequently they would both go to visit their friends Gracie and Harry Baker at their rooms. Sometimes they studied history together there and had a good time. Mrs.Gill decided she didn't want to put up with the noise anymore, so she evicted Gracie and Harry!

Emma and Margaret decided their apartment was big enough, and Mrs. Laramy willing, so the brother and sister moved in with the two girls. Harry slept in an unfinished attic room adjoining their apartment.

Now that it was cold winter weather, their families would take turns bringing in a load of wood for their heating and cooking.Instead of carrying it through Mrs. Laramy's living room, they brought a long rope from home. One of them would stand on the ground and tie the end of the rope securely around a piece of wood. Another would stand at the open window upstairs and pull the piece of wood up the side of the house with the rope, and untie it. A third member of the team would take the piece of wood and stack it neatly against the wall. The person at the window would lower the rope, and repeat the process.

In December Charlie was elected Sunday School Superintendent and started taking that responsibility in January, 1911.

All went well until February when Emma fell sick, not her usual sickness. This was in her chest.When Charlie came by to see her, he was shocked at how ill she was. "Emma, I'm going to get the doctor!" he told her and left.

In a remarkably short time he returned with Dr. Munger. After examining her, the doctor announced, "You're a very sick girl, Emma. You have pleural pneumonia." He prescribed medication for her and spread a plaster of antiphlogistine on her chest and back.

The next day when Charlie went to see her, she lay pale and lifeless against the pillow. The sleeves of her flannel nightgown were pushed up. He found some string and tied a piece around each of her sleeves to keep them down. "I hope you'll soon be well, my dear," he whispered and kissed her hot forehead.

Chapter 20

Word of her illness had been sent to her parents; Ma came, bringing her a new red flannel kimono. Emma was too sick to be moved. It was unthinkable to take her home about six miles with horse and sleigh in the bitterly cold February weather.

Pastor Jessie came to visit Emma and pray with her, and sometimes Sadie came to see her, too.

Margaret and Gracie were good nurses and did what they could for Emma. They took turns, with their teacher's permission coming home during study hall times to check on her. Mrs. Laramy sometimes came up to see her too, bringing beef broth for her to drink.

Charlie came over every day and spent many evenings reading to her if she felt well enough to listen. "Emma, dear, please try to get well. It makes me sad to see you so sick," he whispered close to her ear. He brought Vaseline to put on her chapped lips. He also prayed for her each night before he left.

Ma brought food every week when she and Pa or Lester came to visit.

One day when Sadie was visiting her, she said, "You know, Emma, I think you're almost well enough to come over to our house. In three more days you'll have been sick a month. By that time I think you could come and stay with us, and I'll take care of you until you can go home."

"That sounds good," Emma responded weakly."I would like that."

Three days later, Jessie and Sadie drove up with their sleigh. Sadie helped Emma dress warmly for the move and packed a bag of her clothing. Charlie took Emma up in his arms and carried her down the stairs, and placed her gently in the seat, and wrapped her warmly with a fur robe for the ride. He then climbed in to sit with her, as Jessie and Sadie took their seats.

Emma stayed with Harwoods two weeks, receiving their tender loving care. By that time milder March weather had arrived, and she was a little stronger.

Lester and Charlie came for her in Shepherdsons' cutter on a sunny day in March.Again Charlie picked her up lovingly in his arms and placed her on the seat where Lester had spread a heavy wrap, which they tucked around her.

Little by little Emma regained her strength, but she was not able to go back to school that year. She lost a whole year of school credit. How she appreciated the loving care she received from her friends and family, especially the faithful Charlie! He and his father, Will Leicht and Roy Perry all helped tap the Shepherdson sugar bush that spring.

Sunshine, coming more often in the spring, brought new vigor to Emma as well as new life all around her. One Saturday evening when Charlie came to visit, he asked, "Emma, dear, how are you feeling now?"

"The pain in my chest is gone, except when I cough hard."

"I'll be glad when school is out, so I can see you more often," he said, taking her thin hand in his.

"I'll be glad too."

When school was out, Charlie came up to see her one evening after his chores were done.

"Tell me what you did today," she asked.

"I've been planting potatoes where I plowed last Saturday. We planted the peas first, and they're already starting to come up. It's exciting to see things grow, and it's great to see you looking better and stronger every week!" He held her gently and kissed her tenderly before he left.

Before summer was over, Emma was up and about, doing normal activities. She was still thin, but gaining strength every day. Her cough had almost disappeared.

She and Charlie went with Lester to Camp Houk one day during the summer. It was like a carnival in the woods. Some people camped nearby and enjoyed the delicious water from a bubbling spring. There were concession stands with popcorn, caramel apples, sandwiches, taffy, cotton candy, and ice cream. There was a baseball game, throwing contests, horse shoes, and dancing in the evening.Local Ottawa Indians sold beaded moccasins and leather purses. (Chief Cobmoosa's home was not far away.) Photographers took pictures and produced them within a couple hours. Lester and Charlie enjoyed a game of horse shoes, while Emma ate taffy and watched them play.

After a few hours of walking around and visiting with friends, the three returned home. It was the longest Emma had been on her feet, and she was very tired.

One September evening as Charlie and Emma sat in the lawn swing, Charlie said, "It's wonderful to have you looking and acting more like yourself, but now I'm worried about Mother. She's feeling poorly," he said.

"Oh, I'm sorry. What seems to be wrong?" she asked.

"I asked her that, and she says she just feels sick all over," he replied with a worried look.

"I'll go down to see her tomorrow. Maybe there's something I could do to help her."

"That would be very nice of you, Emma," he said and kissed her tenderly.

The next day Emma took a loaf of bread and a plate of sugar coodies in a basket as she walked to Hulls' house. She was shocked at how thin Mrs. Hull looked with a pale yellow tone to her skin. "Hello, Mrs. Hull," she greeted, taking the lady's hand. "Charlie told me you were sick. Is there something I can do for you?"

"It was so nice of you to come, Dear. Do you think you could give me a bath?" Nellie Hull asked.

"Ye-Yes, of course I can," Emma replied with only a moment's hesitation.

"That would help me feel better."

"I'll go get some warm water."

Charlie was sweeping the rag carpet when Emma came out of the bedroom. Charlie, can you bring a towel, wash cloth, soap and a clean nightdress for your mother? I'm going to give her a bath." She filled a blue and white granite wash basin with warm water from a teakettle on the stove and took it to the room, placing it on a small table near the bed. Charlie brought the requested articles and closed the door, giving Emma a loving look.

She had never bathed another adult before. With a quick silent prayer for help, Emma went to work, knowing that her help was needed. When she had finished, Mrs. Nellie Hull was wearing her clean nightgown and had her hair neatly combed. The lady said, "Thank you, my dear, I feel ever so much better."

Emma patted her hand and said, "You're welcome, Mrs. Hull." When she opened the door, Charlie was playing his favorite record, "I'm Tying the Leaves, So Nellie Won't Go Away." Tears were in his eyes as he held his arms open to embrace Emma.

"Thank you, my dear.Thank you very much," he said, as he held her close, and they cried in each other's arms. Charlie's father soon hired a neighbor lady, Mrs. Adelia Perysian to come and care for his ailing wife.

After Labor Day both Emma and Charlie were back in school, but Charlie was again elected delegate to Annual Conference, this time at North Star. He was elected secretary of the United Brethren Christian Endeavor Association for North Michigan. Conference was held September 13-16, so it was necessary for him to miss a few days of school, but Emma was so proud of him, representing the Sackrider church again at Annual Conference.

She was repeating the eleventh grade, so she had different classmates. One advantage of repeating was that geometry was much easier for her, and she made straight E's for excellent.

Charlie found it very difficult to concentrate on his studies with his mother so ill.

Then on November 2 his brother Jake married Elsie Wolf. Emma didn't know her very well, but she'd heard good things about her.

Ma Shepherdson was with Nellie Holmes Hull on November 30,1911, when Mrs. Hull passed away, just after Charlie's nineteenth birthday. Emma and her family entered the church before the funeral. Charlie and his father and brothers were all using their handkerchiefs as the Shepherdsons stepped up to the casket and joined them in weeping for the beloved lady. Rev. Ida J. Robbins was the pastor who conducted the funeral service at the Sackrider U.B. Church. A horse-drawn hearse led the procession into Hart to the cemetery.

After the funeral Emma took a dish of scalloped potatoes and ham down to the Hull family. Charlie met her at the door. He took the food with thanks and then took both her hands and held them. "I'm so sorry," she said, tears welling up in her eyes.

"Thank you, Dear, and thank you for bathing her before Father had Mrs. Perysian come to take care of her, and thank you for sitting up with me near the end.People have been so kind." He showed her food that others had brought: a cake, pickled beets and sweet cucumber pickles, a beautiful loaf of bread, and some baked beans. "Thank you for the dish of scalloped potatoes.It looks and smells delicious."

Charlie stayed in school until Christmas vacation. Then he dropped out to help at home. Lewie was thirteen and still in the two-room country school. Charlie went to visit Emma one weekend. "It's a good thing Mother taught me how to do some things around the house," he told her.

"What have you been doing this week, Charlie?"

"Lewie helped me do the laundry. Cleaning the house is no problem. Remember I was janitor for years at Sackrider School, but you should have seen the mess I made trying to make cookies," he laughed. "I had flour all over the kitchen and all over me."

With all this experience you'll make someone a good husband," she joked. "Seriously, though, I'm sure your father and Lewie appreciate the sacrifice you're making in staying home at this time."

"Yes, they seem to," he said, taking her in his arms.

"What have you been doing besides house work?"

"Well, in the month of January I've read Genesis, Exodus and Leviticus from the Bible besides some other books. *THE SKY PILOT* is one I enjoyed, and another was *EBEN HOLDEN* by Bacheller. I'm also looking for a job. Two possibilities I've been looking at are operating a roller on a road construction crew and working on the railroad. I've been talking to Roy Perry about what's required to be an engineer. He lent me some of his books on the railroad."

"May God give you wisdom, my dear, to know which direction to take at this time!" Emma responded, giving his face a loving pat.

Chapter 21

One Sunday in late January Charlie and Emma were talking while he took her to town to her apartment. "Emma, what do you think? Pa has decided to have an auction sale."

"He has? What does that mean?"

"It means I'll have less responsibility at home. We've decided to sell my sow, too. Pa's selling his plow and other farm equipment along with corn and some of the other grain we'd saved for seed. Tomorrow Pa and I'll go to town to have sale bills printed up."

"Well, for land's sake! . . . We're having changes in our family too. You know George is going to get married, and Lena and Will are expecting a baby."

"Yes, Lester told me about the wedding. I've seen Lena recently, so I knew about the baby. It's too bad George's wedding'll be so far away, but I guess if Nina lives in Huntington, that's where the wedding should be."

"I know, but I'm disappointed not to be able to go to the wedding. Lester's going, though.He's going to be the best man."

"That's what he told me. I've offered to take him to the train."

"I can't tell you anything, can I?" she laughed.

"Lester and I are good friends, you know. I'm sure I see him more often than you do now that I'm not in school, and you are. If I don't go up to see him, he comes to our house. Sometimes we play Pit or Carroms, and make popcorn. He may stay overnight with me, or I with him."

"I'm glad you and Lester are such good friends."

"This week we felled some trees and cut wood together. Sometimes we go over and help Mrs. Clark since her husband died." (Her lively playing of the organ had added new life to the church services when her family had moved into the Sackrider community.)

"That's very nice of you, but then I knew you were a nice fellow. You're always doing kind things for people."

"Thank you, Dear," he said as he pulled up in front of Mrs. Laramy's house. He put his arm around her and added, "You said you can't tell me anything, but I'd like to have you tell me if you love me."

"Oh, yes, I do love you, Charlie," she said and returned his kiss.

Friday, February second Charlie took Lester to the train, so he could go to Indiana for George and Nina's wedding. Lester said to expect him on the Tuesday train.

Charlie met the train on Tuesday, but Lester didn't come. He visited Emma and her roommates, and was invited to stay for supper.

Wednesday he met the train again, but again no Lester, so he stopped by the apartment. The girls had cooked a soup bone and made soup. "You may as well stay and eat with us," Emma invited. "I'm not feeling well today. I think I'll let you take me home after supper."

"I'll be happy to do that," Charlie replied with a smile.

He carried her luggage as they went down to the waiting sleigh. The weather was cold, but she was warm with Charlie's arm around her.

On Friday Lester arrived on the train, but the weather

had turned ugly. Charlie didn't drive in again to look for him, but Lester found a ride with someone going his way.

On Sunday Charlie told Emma, "When I asked Lester about the reason for his delay in Huntington, he said, 'Her name is Marjorie.' She's a girl he knew when he was down there in college, but now she's got his attention. He seemed excited about her."

"Yes, he's been telling me about her, too. It sounds like it might be a serious relationship."

"Yes, I think so. I wonder if that means another Indiana wedding."

"Oh, I hope not!"

In the middle of February the Hull farm auction sale was held, netting $417. There was a large crowd, and George Hull was satisfied with the result, but Frank, the old horse, was not for sale. Charlie told Emma about it that weekend. "I just didn't have the heart to sell our old Frank. He couldn't do much anymore, and I was afraid someone might misuse him. So I took him for his last walk down the lane."

"What do you mean, Charlie?"

"I mean I shot him. He's worked long enough and hard enough. He deserves a rest."

Lena and Will were living in their house, even though it was not yet finished. However, in February when Lena's time for giving birth was drawing near, Vina insisted on her coming to the Perry house to stay, to be sure she and the baby would be warm enough. On February 22, 1912, a baby boy Willard Shoaf Leicht was born with dark hair and features like his father's. He was the second Shepherdson grandchild and first boy, another very special baby.

Later in February Charlie stopped in to see Emma and her friends at lunch time and joined them. He told Emma that he had gone to a chiropractor about some problems he'd been having with his back. The doctor told him to come back for an adjustment on Friday.

The next time he saw Emma he said, "I have some good news and some bad news."

"Let's have the good news first."

The good news is that I preached at church on Wednesday night, and that Jessie said I should consider going to Fenwick Mission in Ionia County to be their pastor.

"Charlie!Really? I thought Harry Harwood was the pastor there."

"He is now, but they're seriously considering going to the California Conference. I asked Jessie what made him think I could handle the work of a pastor. He said he'd observed me a good deal while he was pastor here last year. He said I'd done a good job as Sunday School Superintendent, that I took other responsibilities in the church, such as helping keep it clean and taking a turn at being a substitute Sunday School teacher or prayer meeting leader. He said he had enjoyed watching me grow as a Christian, and that I have leadership ability that he thinks the Lord can use in the pastorate. He said I should pray about it.

"The Lord did help me preach Wednesday night. I used the text of Matthew 3:2, John the Baptist's message of repentance. It seemed like the Lord was speaking through my mouth. Of course I had studied the passage and prepared a message, but the Lord really did bless me."

"That's wonderful, Charlie!I'm thrilled about the possibility of your being a pastor, but what about schooling and preparation? Will you have to go to Central College?"

"I'd like to, maybe later, but he said the church has a reading course. He'll tell me what books I need or supply them to me. I'll study them and take notes. Then I'll take oral exams on the books. The conference has an examining committee that gives the oral exams."

"So you can study the books while you do the work of a pastor?"

"Yes, the Presiding Elder can issue a Quarterly

Conference License during Quarterly Meeting at our local church. That's temporary. When I work through the reading course, I'll receive my Annual Conference License, and eventually, if I keep on studying, I will be ordained. That will mean a lot of work and study, but you know pastors aren't paid very much."

"The Lord takes care of the sparrows. I'm sure he'll provide for you, especially if you're doing His work. Now for the bad news. What is it?"

"The chiropractor says I have 13 vertebrae out of place. I had my first adjustment Friday, and I have to have many more."

"Oh, Charlie, I'm so sorry. You probably hurt your back carrying me around when I was so sick last winter."

"I doubt it. I've been doing a lot of heavy work, helping Father get ready for the sale, logging and carrying wood. I guess I'll have to get Lewie to do more of the wood carrying.

"Jake's bride, Elsie, is so helpful and generous to us. She brings us a basketful of baked goods once a week, delicious bread and some kind of dessert. She's a very good baker, even if she is only 19."

"I'm glad she's so helpful. I think she sews too."

"Yes, she does.Sometimes when I go over there, she's sitting at her sewing machine or sewing by hand on a dress or curtains."

Rev. Jessie Harwood, Presiding Elder, who was living in the new house he had built in Hart, preached at the Sackrider Church Friday, Saturday and Sunday. On Friday night, March 8, Lewie Hull went forward to receive Christ as his Savior. On Saturday Charlie went to Shepherdsons' house to see Jessie to talk about the reading course. Charlie had already started studying a theology book. That evening, March 9, in the Quarterly Conference business meeting Charles Holmes Hull was granted the Quarterly Conference license to preach.

"This is a very important day, Charlie," Emma told him after the service.

"It's exciting and frightening at the same time, wondering if I will be able to deliver the Lord's message in the right way. It will be very challenging."

The next time he preached was Monday, March 11 on the crucifixion of Jesus, during the revival meeting. The following Sunday Charlie was wearing a new blue serge suit. "Charlie, you look so impressive today. You look like a pastor," Emma commented.

He laughed, "So you like my new suit?"

"Is that it? Well, you do look very nice."

A couple weeks later he said, "Emma, I received a letter from Jessie that the way is clear for me to go to Fenwick."

"Really?That's wonderful, I guess, but it sems so far away. I'll miss you so much."

"I know, my dear. I'll miss you too, but we can write letters. We prayed that the Lord would lead me into what He wanted me to do. Now I must walk through this doorway He's opened for me."

"Emma," he said, a few days later. "I went to vote on Monday about local option. Oceana County voted to go dry by a margin of 865. Isn't that great?"

"Yes, Praise the dear Lord! I wish I could vote. It would've been an 866 majority of people who wanted to live in an alcohol-free county. No, I'm sure many other women would've voted for it too, if they'd had a chance. I'm glad we can vote in church elections," she said with feeling.

"You're right. It isn't fair that women can't vote. I'm sure that'll change. Changing the subject, I wish we'd saved more of our potatoes to sell now. They're selling for $1.17 a bushel. We sold them for 75 cents a bushel back in January. Did I tell you I broke my glasses today?"

"Oh, no!I'd be lost without mine."

"Well, I need them, especially for reading, but not as

badly as you do. I'll get along until I can get some new ones. Would you like to go over to Harwoods' with me to talk about being a pastor and going to Fenwick?"

"Yes, sure. I'll go with you.Just wait until we finish these supper dishes."

"No, Emma, you go ahead," Margaret offered. "We'll take care of the dishes."

"Thanks a lot girls. I really appreciate it," Emma said, taking off her apron and reaching for her coat and hat.

"You'll need your mittens. It's eight degrees above zero even if it is the third of April," Charlie said.

After listening to some information from Rev. Harwood and some pointers about being a pastor, he and Emma enjoyed warm maple sugar. They walked back to Emma's apartment hand-in-hand, talking about their coming separation. After the others had gone to bed, Charlie and Emma sat on the sofa with his arm around her. "Emma, parting with you is going to be the greatest sacrifice I'll make in going to Fenwick, but since the Father is asking me to do it, I'll do it for Him."

"Charlie, I'll miss you so much. You'll write to me, won't you?"

"Of course I'll write and tell you all about it," he assured her.

"What about other girls? There might be some very pretty and jolly girls over there."

He laughed, "Emma, no girl is going to take my attention away from you. You're so precious to me. You're not only beautiful on the outside, you have such a beautiful character to go with it, and you make me laugh. I need that sometimes, and I will never forget that it was you who first told me about Jesus. In time we may be able to do His work together, but for now I must go alone. Will you pray for me, and will you let me go?"

"Of course I will, Charlie," she said, wiping a tear from

her cheek. "You must go and preach and take care of those people over there. I will pray for you and be so proud of you."

"That's my girl," he said and kissed her tenderly. "Now it's time for a schoolgirl to get to bed. Harry's going to let me bunk with him tonight." He held her in his arms as he kissed her goodnight and prayed, "May our Father give us a good night's rest and smile upon our plan to do His will," he prayed before he let her go and went to the attic room to spend the night.

Friday night Emma was at her home when Charlie came to see her. She said, "Charlie, let's go over to see Perrys."

"I can go to Perrys' house any time. I came to see you, my dear."

"Please, I'll go over there with you."

"All right, if it's important to you," he agreed.

When they reached the senior Perrys' house next to Shepherdsons, the door was opened with a cry of "Surprise, Charlie!" His brothers and Elsie were there along with several friends. It was a surprise farewell party for him. There were games and refreshments, and visiting until well after midnight. Emma walked home with Lester and Pearl, and Charlie walked home with his brothers and Elsie. What a delightful surprise party!

Sunday morning Charlie preached at the Sackrider Church from Hebrews 12:1-2 about "Jesus, the author and finisher of our faith." He also signed a temperance pledge that day, that he would abstain from the use of tobacco and alcoholic beverages. Then he took Emma with him to Jake and Elsie's house for dinner.

Wednesday Emma promised herself that she wouldn't cry when Charlie came to say goodbye. Well, it wasn't obvious. She managed to wipe a tear when he hugged her and didn't notice. Oh, it was so hard to let him go! "Charlie, you will write, won't you?"

"Yes, my dear, I'll write and tell you all about what I'm

doing. I'll be taking the train tomorrow. There'll be a little time in Grand Rapids before I go on to Stanton and Fenwick. I'll write you all about it, Sweetheart," he said as he kissed her again and left.

Chapter 22

The following are actual letters or excerpts of letters from Charlie and Emma:

Fenwick, Mich.
April 14, 1912
To My Dear Emma,

Well, Emma, there is a whole lot of satisfaction in knowing you are not forgotten. Write me a long letter as soon as you can and have those other girls write if they don't want to send with you, send separate or any way, but write. I expect these first few days or weeks will be the worst so now is when I want them. The book rack came in good shape. The house here is small, but I guess I have the best room in it—have four windows two looking east; can see two lakes from my room, one takes in a little of the south side of this place, the other is on the other (east) side of the road and a little farther down. (He was living with Mr. and Mrs. Jonas Dull and working for his room and board.) The church is about half a mile south, was painted once, I guess, but it has all worn off. It's neat inside however, nicely papered, has three or four mottos on the walls, an organ and old fashioned, hand made pews, painted a dark brown.

It rained occasionally this morning so there were but about eighteen out, tho I think the average attendance in Sunday School is only about twenty. They elect Sunday School officers for only six months, and they had not been elected for the summer, so it was done this morning; and first thing I knew I was Supt. I was told later that had been so planned before I came to the field—so I think I have something to "blame" Br. J.E. Harwood for.

. . . I'll need a wheel if I go to a school house about 4 1/2 or 5 miles away on Sunday afternoons, which I may do a little later on.

8:30 P.M. Well, another service is gone into eternity. This morning I used Matt. 3:1-12 . . . and this evening I made another try of "Tekel" Daniel 5. God surely blessed me in the services. There were occasional "Amens." And I like to hear them.

Well, now as to my trip, I wish I had written that I would come Friday instead of Thursday, so that I could have stopped with the others and seen Harry. [Lester, Pearl, Sadie and children came as far as Muskegon with me—to see the Harry Harwoods before they left for California.] Stopped in Grand Rapids, did a little shopping. Had to wait at a little dingy depot in Stanton about an hour. They have an engine used for switching in Greenville, and whenever it gets thru with the switching, it hooks to a dirty, smoky, little coach, comes to Stanton, and goes on the Stanton-Ionia Branch; so that is how I arrived. All o.k. right side up—with care. Friday I made two calls in the forenoon and slept a good part of the afternoon. Sat. morning I walked to Fenwick, sent some money to Bro. Mason (at the United Brethren Publishing Dept.) for some books, etc. stopped and peeked around the parsonage a little—that is between here and town –I will enclose a poster that I found there. Came back part way and made another call, staid for dinner—the woman is a Christian, but the man not. He bot Harry's horse and buggy, said he wanted to buy his boy also, but Harry wouldn't sell. He said he always liked Harry and had lots of fun with him—quite a jolly sort of a fellow, I guess. Well,good night, Emma.

Monday morning is here again. You will think I must have been clear played out, having to make so many relays in this note. But I am not.Expect to help wash (launder) in a little while. I'll say "be good to yourself," just to be natural.

Lovingly,
Your Charlie

P.S. There are lots of sore hearts in these parts; three have been laid to rest in the cemetery across the way from the church in the last week.

Tuesday afternoon
Postmark Apr. 17, 1912
My dear Charlie—

I received your long-looked-for, glad-received, splendid, pleasant letter this noon. I'm writing very soon afterward, but you told me to write as soon as I could. You probably have received my other letter by this time, but I couldn't help writing again because I'm so rejoiced to get your letter and know you arrived safely at your destination. I've watched every mail since you went away for some word and went down town last night and then when I didn't get any, I thought something must have happened to you, and now that I have a letter, the girls object to the way I hug them, but they are glad because I'm better-natured. You won't tell that I carried it to school in my waist (blouse) will you? Well, I guess that is enough about one letter when I expect to get ever so many more.

Daggy (Gracie) staid out of school today with the rheumatism. She's going to put a note in mine.

I'm very glad that you got along so nicely Sunday. Oh, I

hope and feel that you will get along finely. You must have been surprised some to have "woke up and found yourself superintendent."

Gracie is "bellering" like a great calf. She called me a nasty, naughty, dirty girl, she did. I didn't do nothing bad either. Now you'll believe it won't you, because you know you said that you would believe anything I told you. Grace had one of her crazy fits on today. (When Harry failed to do his chores, his sister Grace would often do her own and his.Emma did not think this was fair, so she insisted that Harry take responsibility for his own chores. This may have been the reason for the squabble.)

We had a test in physics this morning.

This is a very bright sunshiny day. How very bright the world is anyway with the love of Jesus Christ in our hearts. Yet I get distrustful at times and seem to lack faith.

Yesterday I told Harry to be sure and empty the slop pail before he went to school, and he ran off and left it sitting on the very same spot . . . When he came home from school at night to get his ball glove, and I told him that if he didn't empty it before he went away, we wouldn't get him any supper. He went away and left it, and when he came home to supper, there was more, and he had to get his own supper too.

He is home to supper now, so I'll close for a while.

Well, my dear boy, we have just finished our supper work, and Grace has gone to bed, and Margaret went away somewhere to stay all night, so I'll write a little more. Somehow people seem to feel closer together at night, don't they? Maybe it's just me.I'm noted for strange notions anyway. I suppose you didn't know that.Ha,ha.

The mice are beginning their nightly serenade by the sound. Grace and I played ball last night, and today I'm so sore. Do you find it dull at Dulls'? I hope not. I only wish I could stick my head in at your door about now.

I suppose that I really must go to bed, so that I can get

up early in the morning, so I'll wish you a good night and happy dreams.

From your little girlie,
Emma

P.S. I'm up and about this morning. I dreampt about the young man who has the dime (?) last night. I dreampt he was home, and we had a glorious time.

(Charlie and Emma wrote to each other once or twice a week, but not all the letters are included or excerpted. In June Charlie and the Fenwick Mission rented a tent, and they held nightly tent meetings.)

Fenwick Mission
June 17, 1912
To My Own Dear Emma—

Well, I suppose you have been looking for a letter for some time, and I have been looking for time to write. The meetings have not been large in the line of attendance, but I think they have been good.God has honored our effort . . . We made a mistake in setting the tent where we did—I am largely to blame I guess, so our meetings are not as large as expected.

Tues. 8:00 A.M. I look for a good letter today with a Hart postmark, and Jessie is looking for one also. (Rev. J.E. Harwood was there for Quarterly Meeting.) I am going to help wash today, but the water isn't quite hot, so am at this job. Have had a mess of strawberries. [This new pen works poorly.] Jessie, Br. Shelly & I went fishing a little while in Horseshoe Lake yesterday morning. Had a few little nibbles, but got no fish, as usual.Ha!

The Lord surely blessed me in the service last night—but no one yielded . . . You better not work in the factory next week, or are you doing so at all? I expect to know by 1:o'clock.

Well, it is 11:30, have been running the washer, but Mrs. Dull stopped to get dinner so gave me an honorable discharge. She told me I ought to write that "all things are now ready"—potatoes coming up on the parsonage lot (He had planted them.), strawberries, asparagus, pieplant (rhubarb), horseradish, roses in bloom, etc.etc. Ha, and so I am doing so—sounds very pleasant, doesn't it? My what daydreamd us kids will have.

Jessie is highly pleased with Central College in Huntington, Indiana, the influence, surroundings, location, etc. Wish it was so I could go there this fall. I find that I know but very little—its hard to work on a subject when you know your hearers know more about it than yourself. I am going to try to make up for my lack in the line of sermons by more visiting—see if I can learn more as to the needs, then talk accordingly. Jessie complimented me on my work last night, but because he thot I needed encouragement, I think. I find that a little encouragement means much sometimes. [I Cor. 4:15]

. . . Expect George and his bride are home now, will try and get home while they are there, providing they stay long enough.

. . . Is nearly mail time and I have reached my limit, I guess, so will close and remain

Your loving preacher boy

Charlie

(Near the end of June he took the train home, stopping in Shelby to visit his uncle and aunt and brother Lewie, who was staying with them, perhaps for the summer. The next day he reached Shepherdsons' home. He and Emma spent the evening in the buggy in the buggy shed. Pearl made several trips past the buggy shed, watering the garden during the evening.)

July 18, 1912

Dearest Charlie,

. . . George got the best joke on me last night.I told him to be sure & bring me a letter, and he said that if he did, it would be opened when I got it. So when he got home, I was washing dishes, and he came in and showed me a letter and covered up all but the name Shepherdson, and I thot I knew the writing, so I dried my hands and went to read it and sure enough it was open, and a money order in it and I couldn't understand it, and I went to unfold the letter, and I thot it pretty thin, and then I glanced at the envelope and saw who it was addressed to. Then I demanded my own and of course got it.

George and Nina are going down to Aunt Lucy's to supper, and I'm going along and get an apron and some other stuff, so I suppose it's goodbye 'till Camp Meeting.

With lots of love from

Emma

Shanty Plains (Fenwick)

Sun. 9:30 P.M.

Postmark Jul. 22, 1912

Well, Dearest, another day is nearly complete, and Oh! So much as it has meant to some.Just after we had family worship this morning, the little girl from across the road came over and said, "Wallace D. died this morning." I saw him at work yesterday, apparently well. In bed this morning he awakened the family . . . when they reached the bed, he expired—leaves a widow and some small children. The family have been quite regular at church. They want a certain old friend of the family to preach, but have been unable to locate him. If they don't find him, it falls my lot. It is to be Tuesday P.M. So I could not go to G.R. as I had thot—guess it is best you planned on going the other way.

. . . Well, it's bedtime, and I feel like going to bed, as I will have to get busy and study for a new duty, so as to be ready if they want me. I will save the rest until I see you, I guess.

Your own loving Charlie

Chapter 23

Emma and her friend Edna Robbins, the pastor's daughter, went by train to Carson City. Mr. Will George met them at the station and took them to Culy's grove north of Carson City on the east side of Mt. Hope Road. There they met Charlie, who also attended the Camp Meeting for ten days.The letters begin again.

Fenwick, Mich.
Thurs. 5:00 P.M.
Postmark Aug. 16, 1912
My Dearest Emma—
Received your lovely letter in due time.

. . . Tuesday morning I went over to Orleans—5 miles—to call on Bro. Clawsons, fine people. (five miles to Clawsons' seven to Orleans) They lost a daughter recently—perhaps I told you of it—25 years of age. I had never seen her. Such a glorious Christian experience she had. She saw glory in a dream before she died and told them how grand it was.

. . . Guess I'll have to go to the Congregational circuit Sunday. (He was sometimes asked to substitute for his friend Rev. Alexander, the Congregational pastor at Sheridan and Sidney.) Pray for me.And I have written the

Potterville folks that I expect to be out there next week, so don't know when I will find time to write you another letter. But just remember whatever comes that out here in the middle of the state there is a heart that beats true for you within the person of Your preacher boy,

Charlie

Hart, Mich.

Sept. 8, 1912

My own Sweetheart -

. . . O say, just think I'm going to live with Lena and Will and Willard this winter. Won't that be nice? Will is going to work for Van Allsburg, and they are going to move to town for the winter anyway.

We had a prayer meeting this morning before Sunday School. (This may have been when the pastor was preaching at the other church on the circuit.) Mrs. Clark led it, and a very helpful lesson to me it was. She read the 14th chapter of St. John and asked us to choose some verse and talk about that in testimony. I took the one "Let not your heart be troubled neither let it be afraid." What a comfort there is in that verse, that if we only trust in Him, we need have no fear, that He will provide what is best for us to have. God help us to be patient and have faith, oh, so much faith.

Well, I must tell you about Grace's birthday party. It was a surprise on her, and it certainly was. I was over to Lena's, and Lester came over and got me. The crowd was there before we got there . . . Herman Andrews came up and offered his services, and so he got us some water and talked to us. They began playing "Snap and Ketchum" right in front of us, and someone chose Herman, and he told them that he couldn't go because he was engaged. Grace and I wanted to watch the fun and still not be in the game, so we kept some food on our plates, so that folks would see us eating and not choose us. Well, I really never realized how silly those kissing games were 'till last night . . . Herman said that if he wanted to kiss a girl, that he would go to her house. That was my sentiment too. . . .

I don't feel a bit good this morning. I wish I had Sombody's lap to sit on and Somebody's arms to put around me and Somebody's neck to put my arms around and Somebody's face to look at and Somebody's shoulder to lay my head on.

. . . Lewie intends to stay at Jake's and go to Sackrider School this year, he says Miss Roberts and Ethel Miller are going to teach. They begin today.

Elsie and Jake were to church a week ago yesterday, and I sat by Elsie in S.S. and I heard and saw Lewie pointing out the two sisters.Ha,Ha.

. . . George's daddy-in-law (Mr. Steman) has a new auto, and George runs it some of the time. He said that he ran it 28 mi. per hour over rough roads. Did I tell you that Prof. Mummart and Father Steman had secured a scholarship for George?

My dear, I <u>must</u> close and get ready for school. So with lots of love,

I am your own Emma

Fenwick, Mich.
Sunday 2:00 P.M.
Postmark Sep. 30,1912
Greetings to my Darling Emma—

Well, dinner isn't quite ready, and I can't wait any longer before writing you, so here goes.I arrived right side up with care. Had a pleasant tho lonely trip. I couldn't help wishing you were beside me. (He had made a trip to Hart by train on his return from attending Annual Conference at Bates, near Traverse City.)

O, say! When I arrived in town I went to the store-post office to leave my suitcase overnight, and I found a letter from Bowman with a $10.00 check—missionary money (Since Fenwick was a mission, he received some mission money from time to time from Rev. Bowman, Mission Secretary for the Conference.) and a letter from Alexander with $5.00 in it. So you see that Congregational trip gave the highest wages I ever got. . . Guess I will send Sister Robbins $1.00.I think perhaps I will send the check to Pa and have him put it in the bank for me toward a school fund.

. . . I read of a man trying to quit smoking. He got so hungry for it that he took three cigars to a friend who smoked them while the first man sat so the smoke was blown in his face, and said it was about as satisfying as he imagined kissing your best girl's picture might be. Ha! Well, I"ll just say I don't see how Lester gets along. Perhaps I had better close now, darling, and brush up a little . . . for this evening's service.

Lovingly your own
Preacher kid, Charlie

Hart, Mich.
Oct. 13, 1912
My own Sweetheart,

This is Sunday evening, and I am at home.Pa's going to town in the morning, so I'm going with him. Vina and I went down to see Mrs. Miller this afternoon . . . She does beautiful fancy work. She said that she had every letter that Henry ever wrote to her. . .

Lena and Will have got moved at last. (They moved into an upstairs apartment over the grocery store they managed.) I stayed there with them Thurs. night.I get my mail with Will now. Dearest, I didn't know but you had deserted me. I looked for a letter on every mail from Tues. noon until Friday noon. Then I was in the bedroom and when I came out, there was a letter on my plate. I wasn't long in getting it.

We were eating dinner and I got up to get some salt, and Lena and Will were jabbering, and Will jumped up and came over and said, "Shut your eyes." I shut them, and he kissed me and said, "That's from Charlie." But I know it wasn't.

. . . We have our silo filled. Did you hear that Lester got his hand cut? When he was cutting Perrys' silo corn with his patent machine, he went to get some corn out of the way, and the front end of the machine hit a stone, and the knife came up and took him on the thumb and cut a gash shaped like a square "U" and an inch each way. It's much better now. That was a week ago.

You asked me if I got any work at the factory. I worked Friday forenoon and all day Sat. and earned about $1.60 anyway. I husked corn a little and pitted peaches a little and sorted plums and worked on time.I could work up there nights some, but it is so cold and damp that I feel as if I ought not to.

. . . I'm making me a new hat . . . from an old waist and a little du-dad that is about 50 years old and a piece of trimming and a button that Aunt Em gave me. I can economize on my clothes if I can't peel potatoes as thin as some folks. . .

I'm awful glad that Mrs. Dull is so good to you. The dear woman. But I'm afraid that I am a little jealous of her. But then, perhaps there will be years and years, O happy years.

My soul feels good tonight, and I have faith to believe that He will bless my darling as He sees best. Ma thinks that I had better go to bed. So good night, my Own Dear Boy

Emma

Fenwick Mission

Sun. 7:00 A.M.

Postmark Oct. 14, 1912

My own dear Sweetheart—

The sun is brightly shining this morning, and I feel good in my soul. I was lying abed hugging a pillow and found but small satisfaction in that, so decided to dress and start a note for you. This room is rather chilly, but I believe I could get my arms warm if you were here. I don't know how fast the next three years are going to go, but somehow it seems a long six months since I was where I could see you every other day or so. And yet again it doesn't seem very long ago that Mother was sick and you helped me sit up. It has now been a few days over a year since she she was taken sick. Yesterday I got my diary to look at a certain page in April—I kept reading . . . I also see that for the 17th it said, "Emma and I went out to the gully after school." Do you remember that? O such times as we children have had! Praise the Lord for it all! Well, Darling, breakfast is ready and after that I must brush up a little for the services, so with lots of love I will close for the present.

(Later after a discussion of some of his church people and their spiritual problems and progress—)

. . . As Jesus said once, "The multitudes go the other way," but if we can get once in a while, one here and there, started for Heaven, we can praise God just the same. Oh, Emma dear, it is a large vineyard God has, and if it is His will that you and I work together, we may be able to do a little toward helping one here and there. It is certain we will not have to look far to find the work to be done . . .

Tomorrow I expect to start into an eight acre field to husk corn at five cents per bushel—that is a big price, but I expect the corn is poor. That is the reason I wanted to finish this note to my sweetheart tonight. Somehow, darling, the more I see of these girls, the more I love you. As I get better acquainted with them I find myself thinking, "Emma would be better than that" or "do better than that." . . . But must say good night and be up early.

Lovingly your Charlie

Hart, Mich.
Oct. 27, 1912
My blessed Sweetheart,
This is a beautiful Sunday afternoon, and I'm as happy

as I can be [without you] . . .

I stayed down Sat. and Lena got my skirt cut and fitted . . . I'd like to get my dress done to wear Fri. night. The H.S. chorus is going to sing at the Lecture Course . . .

Ma and Pa went over to Trommaters' to dinner today, and Lewie and Gertha Eisenlohr were here. I wore my new hat today.

I went to see Mrs. Hutchins Sat. and she advised me to go to Normal if I could but said by careful study and observation I could learn a great deal myself, and she is going to have a reading circle this winter, and I could have the benefits of that, and she said I might get time off and visit the grades, which I think I will do.I hope to hear your opinion this week . . .

I'm invited to a Huskin' Bee Mon. night. The Congregational Christian Endeavor are giving one for non-residents. . .

I'm kind of anxious for Christmas to come myself. Can you imagine why? Of course you are planning to be here at Commencement. It would hardly be Commencement for me without you. . .

I'll close and remain
Your own Emma

At Dulls' Sunday 4:30
Postmark Oct. 28, 1912
My own Dearest Emma –

. . . How easy it is to sing praise to the Lord when things seem to be working nicely! Well, I am much elated over the work here, so I guess I might as well write of that now as later. I rode to Orleans this morning and preached there to about 15—fair for a start I think. (He had reopened the church at Orleans.) Came back part way and stopped at Bro. Clawson's for lunch. One woman said, "I'll say this much, you did well, and I enjoyed your talk." Well, you know those things spur one on. I tried to talk from I Cor. 4:15, using Ezekiel 3:15-21 as a lesson—stole it from Bro. Jessie . . . I did get fired up on that line of thot somehow—praise the Lord! And now back to my subject again—after lunch, came to Shanty Plains and started Sunday School . . . When teachers took classes, Edith was in mine and one girl in the Intermediate, so we doubled up and in about 10 minutes I had a class of 15—after they all arrived. Forty four total present—most since I have been here. That is in answer to prayer. We have been praying, and God answered . . .

But how I wish you were here to help. We have a class here for which we are having a hard time to find a teacher . . . Well, last Wednesday I rode over to Orleans (on his bicycle) and helped at the church some more—put up stove pipe etc. The windows are not all washed and the gallery isn't cleaned, so expect to go again this week.Staid at Bro. Clawson's Wed. night and went to Belding Thur. . . .

Well, Darling the Lord has been very good to us and given us many precious seasons together, and tho He may lead us in ways that are far apart for a few years, yet we can praise Him that it is as well with us as it is!

I don't know about not taking Normal.It is different to be sure, than as if you planned on teaching several years as did Lena.If that were your plan, of course the Normal would be a good investment. But it would be pleasant to have you down to Central two years from now; while you would be teaching if you spent another year at Hart. And I more than half believe that you don't intend to teach more than six or eight years.I'll pray that He may direct you in deciding . . .

Well, Sweetheart, I guess I am at the end of my string, so will have to close and keep my word by writing to Jessie. Lovingly your Charlie,

Boy preacher

Chapter 24

Hart, Mich.

Dec. 12, 1912

Dearest Charlie,

. . . We are reading a story in German . . . I cried tonight because the right man does not get the girl he wants in the story. O, Sweetheart, I'm looking forward to a jolly time Christmas vacation. We are going to have two whole weeks vacation . . . I'm looking for my Sweetheart and Lester for his . . .

Jessie remarked (in Quarterly Meeting) that Bro. Charlie was doing very good work and that his heart was in his work . . .

O, darling, I can hardly wait for Christmas, or rather the day when my lover will come. . . O, I feel as if I would like to have you here right now.

I would not let Roy Perry smoke and walk up the street both with me yesterday, and he chose to walk with me rather than smoke.

Sadie and the children were out to Quarterly Meeting. Sat. in the night Ma and Pa and Sadie were all sick. I'm so afraid that Pa will choke sometime that I don't know what to do. Ma doesn't hardly dare to go to sleep. The cold weather seems to choke him up. O, dear, oh, dear, I love my Daddy. Well, anyway my Heavenly Father is loving and kind and He knows best.

Darling, I cannot write anymore tonight, so
Good night own dear Boy,
Lovingly Emma

(The letters resume after his Christmas visit.)

Shanty Plains, at Dulls'
Mon. 9:30
Postmark Jan. 6, 1913
My own Darling Emma,

Well, here I am on the job again. Earl (Trommater) and I had a pretty good visit about everything in general and girls especially. We talked about Nate and Lucile, as I guess most everyone does . . . Mrs. Andrews sat in the seat ahead of as far as Muskegon. The train was well loaded—we stood up from Muskegon to G.R. (Grand Rapids)– students going back to school. We ate dinner at the English Kitchen in G.R.—pretty good chuck for 20 cents. . .

Dr. Munger . . . gave me a bottle of white candy (sugar pills saturated with liquid medication) which he said he thot would help my back . . .

(Lester had gone to visit Marjorie because she wanted to spend Christmas with her family, so he had asked Charlie to do the Shepherdson farm chores while he was at home.)

O, yes!I told Edith about having a chore job while at home. She said, "That is some more of your goodness—you must let people pile the work on you there as well as here."

"Oh, well, I didn't mind that," I answered, "As long as Lester left his sister at home."Ha!

"O, that's it," she said."Of course not."

. . . Well, I must draw this to a close. Hoping to receive a letter soon from my Sweetheart. I also expect to receive a cap, but I won't accept a mitten from you. (To give someone the mitten meant jilting them.)

Lovingly yours and yours to be—Charlie.

Hart Mich.

Jan. 26, 1913

My own dear Charlie—

I received your comforting letter Friday. Indeed I have longed and longed for you this last week, but the Heavenly Father has been all sufficient. Three weeks ago today Pa was taken so much worse, and two weeks ago today was when he wanted us to pray with him, and a week ago he left us. The last week he couldn't talk much, at the last he could only say single words. But he seemed to be waiting for Sun. Almost every day he would ask if it was Sun. We had the funeral at the church Tues. P.M. Rev. Maltman (from Elbridge Methodist Church) preached a good sermon from "The steps of a good man are ordered by the Lord." Psalm 37:23

. . . One day when I was down to Vina's she was laughing and told me what Roy had said, "Em will just worship Charlie."

And Vina said, "I don't worship him (Roy).Ha, ha."I don't expect to worship any man, but I know that I love him now as much as I dare to. (I don't blame Edith for liking you.)"

. . . Semester examinations are this week, and I haven't been to school since Christmas, I went to see Mr. Jensen, and he said that I had better take the exams for convenience sake, but I needn't worry about them for he would see the teachers about my work and I could bank upon due consideration and allowances for my work.

. . . How I look and long for your letters, your dear letters!

Good night my Own True Love—Emma

At Dulls'
Tues. 3:00 P.M.
Postmark Feb. 18, 1913

To the sweetest Girl on earth—

I love you, Emma dear. I just received the sweetest letter ever, then I thot of you without any. I surely felt cheap last Thursday—as I started for the box 3/8 of a mile away I saw the carrier just turning away from the box, so I did not get your letter mailed. Your letters are so dear—second only to Jesus' love letters to me. His are so sweet I like to read them over and over—I read your several times. I thot perhaps as other things had developed perhaps Lester would go out to Huntington before June. (Lester planned to be married in June.) Well, I am glad he intends to take you along—you will of course go Saturday. I had planned on slipping out home Friday, get there at 7:30 just in time to see you graduate . . .

O, I thank my Father for bringing your sweet influence to bear upon my life.

The Holy Spirit is talking to the hearts of men—middle aged men who have families and we are holding on (with prayer) for Almighty God to shake their sandy foundations still more. He is answering.O, my loving Father, Crown Jesus, my elder Brother, Lord of all.Glory!

. . . Really, Darling, I have hoped of late that we would not have to wait more than eighteen months—let us say months. It sounds shorter. You will tell me what you think of that suggestion.Emma, I love you, and am asking Father about it.

Remain ever your own
Charlie

Hart, Mich.

Feb. 25, 1913

My own precious Charlie –

It is now 9:10 P.M. I have part or most of my chemistry lesson, but I'm so sleepy I can't study.I suppose you are looking anxiously for an answer to your letter.

Really, Dearest, it seems a most perplexing problem. You know I want to do what is best, and it would be glorious to be together so soon. What is bothering me is what I'm going to do next year. I wish I had not given up the Reading Circle course, and I'm wondering if I couldn't study up and take the exam next fall—and again I've thot of learning the dress maker trade, and in that way I could always help and be with you too. I wish you would write your opinion, Dear.

I have almost quit worrying, however, and decided to leave it with the Father.

Will & Lena went to the Methodist revival last night.Willard can walk alone for about six or seven feet . . .

I must close, but remain true to my far away Sweetheart

Emma

(Postcard enclosed with letter) Tuesday 7:00 A.M.

Postmark May 6, 1913

Dear Emma—Don't know whether I will have time to write a letter today or not so will try this. I shoveled on the road Fri. oh, yes, Thurs. also, and expected to work again yesterday, but it rained. The gang has not come this morning yet, but it's nice and they may. Frank came over, and he and I papered for Aunty Dull yesterday, so I failed to write you. He is a good boy. I told Aunty Dull I might get homesick and want to come back here this fall instead of Central.Time will tell. Had excellent services Sunday at both points. Have been having some trouble with a flat (bicycle) tire. Expect Frank back today to finish papering.

(Letter)

My Own Darling Emma:

Please read the card first.

It is now 7:35 A.M. and it doesn't look as if the road boss was coming, so I will now start to write on a little larger scale. I love you dearly.Truly if it were not for your lovely letters, I could not stay here . . .

Bro. Dull and I shoveled on the road, Bro. Guernsey was on with his team—the other team was Sister Drake's - Charlie (16 years) drove it; the boss is a Methodist Episcopal, so you see we had a pretty good gang—no swearing or any such . . .

Sweetheart, I heartily wish I might have been there for you to cry on my shoulder. If I had been there, you would not have cried. It hurts me to think of your being sick; and then I wish more than ever that I might be near you . . . Yet we cannot expect roses without thorns. You said you feared you would be a burden, but, Darling, you know I would love to have the privilege of bearing such a burden. Yet, I know as do you, that your helpfulness would be of untold worth; that is saying nothing of the joy and comfort of being in each other's company. You say you plan on it—I am glad you do—I plan on it much.Every old catalog I see I am looking up for furniture. I daydream about seeing you in the little white parsonage down here . . .

I don't believe I can keep it to myself any longer.I have thot of it ever since Jessie was here and suggested my taking a work (church) next year. Perhaps you have read it between the lines before this.It has been in my mind and you know I can't keep a secret. I have said to Aunty Dull, and maybe I have said it to you that I would not go out another year on to a field alone. [I may have to take it back.] But really, Emma, I have thot that if things should work out in such a way that it would seem wise for me to take a field next year, that I would have to come after you about holiday time or before. Don't you think I have done well in keeping such thots to myself so long? So I would like to come back here this fall and then bring you along. You said in your last letter you would like to come, and I know you would like it here . . . I thot I would not tell these thots to you 'till June, but I could not keep them any longer. O, I love you dearly. Perhaps if I told you my pocketbook has only 8 cents in it, you would get all out of the notion of wanting to live at Fenwick. But there is $3.00 coming from the highway.

We finished papering the front room yesterday, and were going to paper the bedroom today The strips are short, so I believe I will go down and try it myself. (Frank had not come.) I could not help but think yesterday that maybe the parsonage will need papering sometime. So I will learn how. Dreaming got Joseph into trouble, but don't let these daydreams of mine draw your attention away from school. I tried to keep from telling you, but failed. I fail in so many things. If you really knew what a failure I was, you would turn your attentions to Herman. But I am quite careful to keep my failures as much out of your sight as possible because I am selfish enough to want you; hence will do my best to make you think I am a very desirable person.

I hear Aunty Dull tearing paper, so I must be going.Will bring this volume to a close. But sweetheart, I love to receive long letters from you. Your last one was so loving.

Sincerely I love you,

Amen, Charlie

Hart, Mich.

May 30, 1913

My own Neglected Sweetheart,

I received your card today and your letter Wednesday. How I did enjoy it! Oh, how I realized the truth of Portia's statement where she said, "Love is blind and lovers cannot see the pretty follies themselves commit." You poor blinded boy. Still I hope that you will always be so . . .

I did some sewing while I was (at Harwoods').I would like to finish my graduating dress tomorrow.I am staying down so that Lena can work in the store tomorrow if they need her. Lester says that he would rather have you, (for best man at his wedding), but of course it is not compulsory. Of course I would be glad to have you come as soon as you can . . .

I probably won't go home again until after school is out. A week from tomorrow is the Senior Picnic, and I think 2 weeks from Sunday is a drill at the Baptist Church, and I'm instructing them, and if you should come the Sat. before that, Sadie said "You can spoon in our gully." Ha,ha.Do you know anything about that? . . .

O, Sweetheart, I can't help loving you. I have told Sadie quite a few things, and she doesn't see the need of us waiting 40 years. She says that I am not quite as old as she was when she was married, but fully as capable of caring for a household, if not more capable, <u>she</u> said. Well, anyway, I'm glad of one thing, you generally eat most anything that is set before you . . .O, I'm thankful for a whole lot of things, for your own dear self especially. It seems as if I can hardly wait 'till I see your dear face again.I hope that it will never be necessary for us to stay apart so long again.

Edith Button has me married to a preacher in her (class) prophecy, she told me, and I asked her how she happened to think that, and she said she just guessed. Ha, ha. However, Rev. Clapp says that nothing ever <u>just happens</u>, but that a Divine Hand plans everything. . .

O, say, Dearest, when you are home, if we decide to live together next year [Doesn't that sound good to you? It does to me.] Well, if we decide, we'll spend a long time together looking through the catalogues and estimate how much it will take to start us out. Really and truly how can one think about anything else? . . .

With lots of love to my own dear preacher Boy from
Emma

Chapter 25

My own Darling Emma—

. . . My Darling, I am disappointed. I received a card from Rev. J.E. Saturday stating that the Quarterly here would be June 28. So that settles my coming to see you. If I staid (after the Christian Endeavor Convention in Huntington just before the wedding) to see Lester threshed (married), I would not get away from Huntington 'till the 17th. It's almost necessary that I be here the Sunday before Quarterly, and I know you would not want me to come home just for three days—it would be just an aggravation. So Dearest, I guess it means to wait 'till it's a full six months—'till the 30th. I am disappointed, and am sure you will be . . .

Dearest, which would you rather have, a ring or a watch? . . . We will have two or three things to talk over after this six months separation.I love you dearly.

Darling, those extra two weeks will go quickly, so please don't feel very sad over the disappointment. We will put in good time when I do come and make up as best we can for lost time. No lost time.I owe it to the people and to God. So Goodbye, Sweetheart for this time—

Your own Charlie

Hart, Mich.
June 3, 1913
My own Sweetheart –

. . . I'm so sorry too that you are so disappointed about coming. I tried not to cry, Dear, but when I had finished reading my letter Lena said, "Isn't he coming?"

I had to tend to Willard right away, so I didn't have time to cry out loud. Well, when you do come, you'll have to stay a good long time.

Now Dearest, about the watch or ring proposition—I don't care in the least for any ring except a wedding ring, and I don't believe I'll need that right away, do you? And I don't want you to get me any watch because you can't afford it. I don't want you to give me anything for graduating present except a good lot of loving when you get home. Another thing if I were you, I wouldn't buy her anything of that sort until I found out whether her mother would allow her to receive it.Ha,ha.Better wait, hadn't you, Dear?

. . . Bessie Waterman brought me up a lovely silver souvenir spoon last night for my graduating present.I have my (class) will all finished also. It is in for final corrections now. I'll close now and write up my Chemistry "Table of Contents" but loving you dearly and longing to see you and all the rest that goes with seeing you,

I am your own Emma

(Lester and Marjorie's wedding was in conflict with Emma's graduation, so Charlie went to Huntington to be Lester's best man and missed Emma's graduation entirely.)

East Lansing
Tuesday, June 17, 1913
To My own lonely Loved one.

Well, here is Tuesday again. Last week at this time I was

in Fenwick ready to take the train, and today I am at Jake's and Ayres. (His brother Jake and wife had moved to Lansing, and Orville Ayres was a cousin.)

I don't know where to begin the story. Had good convention—well attended.Raised a subscription of $172.00 for the Medical Missionary Fund.

Well, yesterday was a fitting climax. It was the mostest high toned affair I ever got mixed up into. Everything went off fine however—even the old shoes.Miss Imo and I attended them. The newlyweds sat at one end of the table, and we at the other.

The first course was a plate with two strawberries, a few cherries, and a little sugar. Next was potato, meat, and biscuit. Then the salads. Later ice cream and cake and last was Lester's candy . . .

Orville asked me if I cared for a trip with him in the auto, so now it is 10:45. Lester gave me a card yesterday to mail to you which I haven't had a chance to do yet. He wrote it on the train. I saw them safely deposited at Montgomery, but I came on thru to Jackson and then changed to the electric line and arrived at East Lansing about 11:30 last night. I was not sure which house Jake's were in, so went to Orville's last night, and lo, when I went up to bed, there was Lewie. He just came last evening.

It was a nice trip all around, but I don't need to tell you who I sighed for . . .

Well, the week is going rapidly, and so will next and then—. I love you dearly and long to see you. All are well and trust you are. With lots of love to the sweetest girlie on earth—the one I dearly love,

Sincerely your Charlie

Hart, Mich.
Thursday P.M.
Postmark June 27, 1913

My own Darling,

Only four more days until I can see you and hear you and feel you again.I've been in bed all day, but I'm sitting propped up on the couch now. It seems, Sweetheart, as if I want you the most when I'm sick . . . But O, how I long for your care and presence! . . .

I expect to be at the station Mon. evening with the slowest horse we possess, so do not fail me. I hardly know whether it is safe for me to go to the station or not.

As ever your own Emma

(The letters resume after that long-awaited visit.)

Shanty Plains
7/14/13
To my own Darling Emma—

Hello, Dear—I love you today more than ever before, I think. This morning Paul Brown came down and said they needed help to haul wheat, so I went up there. I came away with a dollar bill for the Lord. I thank Him for the physical strength He grants me. . .

I saw something in G. Rapids Saturday that I had never saw before tho I suppose it is common—a woman by the railroad picking up pieces of coal . . .

When I changed cars, when I went to dinner, yes, most of the time I thot "Next time I don't expect to do this alone."I did not go up by the furniture stores, but Bro. Clawson takes the *PRESS*, so I may see the ads occasionally. . . He is a very confiding man and a very good man . . . We have excellent visits. I told him that I expected to go home in Sept. after a wife, and he approved of it. Aunty Dull and Uncle Jonas were both pleased. I don't mean to tell everyone yet. Ha.I think tho that after while I will ask Sister Clawson if she wants to sell her horse . . .

I expect next week at this time I will be getting ready for Camp. Will likely go Tuesday.Will J.E. bring his tent? . . .

I love you dearly and trust these two months will go quickly. Good bye for the present.Received collars today O.K.

Your own Charlie

Hart, Mich.

Friday A.M.

Postmark Jul 18, 1913

My own Darling—I was so glad to get your card and letter . . . I spent $.50 for a dozen pint cans, and Ma and Vina and I went raspberrying last Wed. and I canned up five pints of raspberry jam for us, say, Dear, it's so much fun to do things for us . . .

Adelia told me yesterday that there were pillows there that we could have, and lots of other things. (Charlie's father had married Adelia Perysian, a divorcee, in the spring) . . .

I'm expecting to get some toweling next time I go to town, and I've been looking at some sheets in a catalogue that I think are a bargain, and so does Ma.Lena thinks I am one foolish girl.

Jessie is going to take his tent, but Sadie is going too. She is going to leave Anna here, and I expect Ruth at Trulls' . . .

I love to have you write often, Dearest.I must close and get to work, from your own little girl.

In Camp Meeting Grove
Thurs. 2:00 P.M.
Jul. 25, 1913
To my own Darling Emma—

Glory to God for victory!Eight or nine at the altar last night . . .Charlie Harwood and I boarded ourselves 'till Sat. when Aunty Dull, Sr's. Brown and Drake, Mrs. Lutherloh, and Nellie Conklin [girl of 12] came. Now they cook for us.

Br. And Sr. Durham, evangelists are here from Kansas. We have read of them in the *CONSERVATOR.*They work together. He leads singing, exorts, gives invitation, the two sing together, but she is an ordained preacher . . . She beats anything I ever heard . . .

I love to receive your letters when that is the best that can be done, but I am looking forward to the time when I may receive you; yourself, bag and baggage.I am hungry for a home. I love you dearly and need you to help me. All sounds as if I were very selfish, doesn't it? But I trust we may work together for the glory of God.

If we keep humble He may be able to use us to the saving of many souls. We live, 1st to get ready for heaven and 2nd to help others to get ready. But I trust we may be able to work in an easier, happier manner and perhaps do more good by working together.Father bless our fellowship to thy glory!

Well, Darling, I must close and get ready for service, but I love you very dearly and anxiously await Sept. 18. . .

Love to you from Charlie

Chapter 26

Hart, Mich.
July 29, 1913
(Sent to Carson City % Stephen Culy)

My own dear Charlie;

I received your dear letter last night, and I had to read it three times and some of it again, before I could go to bed.

I'm glad you are having a "lovely time without me" Dear, but I'm with you in thought. What a splendid time we will have next year maybe . . .

Earl (Trommater) and Herman and Margaret were up to dinner Sun. and stayed until 9:00, and Margaret stayed all night because it was wet. We swung out in the barn, and Herman said the swing board was too short and said to have a longer one before they came again . . .

I went to the store last night and bought a couple pairs of pillow cases, and Marjorie is going to embroider a pair of them for me, and Grace has promised to embroider a pair, so we will have two pairs of embroidered ones anyway.

I canned 13 quarts of cherries last Sat. for Pat Perysian, and I got $.50 for it . . .

I have one of the quilts all set together, and I had enough

left of the goods to make meinself an apron. Della says that her new sewing maching sews just fine.

O, Charlie, my own Darling, how can I ever wait, and yet it is so near. I believe that I do need someone about your size to take care of me. When Mame was here, and I was sick, she asked me what I would do at such a time when I was married. I told her that I had someone who would take good care of me. [I remember when I watched you put your mother's rubbers on over her shoes for her before going out in wet weather. I was impressed.] Say, I got a lump in my throat now.What makes it? . . .

I'll close and write a little to Sadie.

With lots of love from

Your own Emma

P.S. P.M. I have just ordered 10 yds. of toweling and 4 sheets from Sears and Roebuck. I'm going up to Clarks' & maybe we will go raspberrying tomorrow. I love you Dear, and I love to make plans for us. - Emma

Fenwick, Mich

Tues. P.M.

Postmark Aug. 13, 1913

My very own Emma—

I received the sweetest letter today from my Sweetheart so surely I ought to be happy and I am . . .Well, when I read your dear note over three thimes this P.M. I just felt so good that I could not study theology. I could not get my mind down to the book or its contents. So I took my letter down and read parts of it to Aunty Dull, and she rejoices with me.She is a dear soul . . .

I suppose before you receive this you will have the quilts all tied. You will surely get roasted. Maybe it's best I am not going to be there, or they would be carrying us around the yard on a dry good box or some such performance. The worst of it is you will have to take all of the jokes of these few weeks alone . . .

It's just like your mother to be getting rugs etc. ready for you. (Bessie Shepherdson sewed narrow strips of rags together and wound them into balls. Then she took them to a weaver, and had them woven into enough strips several inches wide for a 9x12 rag carpet for them.) Rug made, fruit canned, and quilts to be tied; it surely looks or sounds as if something was going to happen. Father is surely graciously opening the way . . . Did I tell you that I gave Uncle Jonas a dollar to buy sugar with? Aunty Dull is putting up some nice apple jelly for us. She told me today that she had rags and Sr. Riker has a loom . . . Some strips for the kitchen would be nice. That sounds a little as if I expected we would come back here. Well, I am a little inclined to expect it. Father's will, not mine.

We won't need a heating stove right on the start, and unless we could get a little rake off, it would not be necessary to buy that when we get the other stuff, for we could send right back after, it, you know, when we get ready for it. Heater and rug off from our list makes $18.00 less. What I was thinking is that the more money we have, the easier it will be to buy a rig should we come back here. For I told Jake to keep that $30 unless we really needed it, for that will about pay up what I owe him. . .

Think I will go to the much advertised "Man from Michigan" in Greenville.It's an all wool store and good suits for $10. and $12.Horace (Shinabarger) had a nice suit from there that he got recently for $10. This much is certain, Emma dear, we will not worry in the least, for Father is still at the helm. We asked Him for guidance, so we will leave it in His care.

Dearest, I love you and anxiously await the day when I may have you indeed. How is your graduating present wearing? Must be nearly gone, paying for rugs, etc. I ordered my books of Mason and have a dollar check I could enclose if you need it. They are working on the road somewhere north; guess I'll see if they need any help. I have been thru theology once—I took notes, so I can review it quickly now.It must be drill and review, for that is the most important exam. . .

I praise the Lord every day that He ever put it into your heart to love me. I agree that nothing just happens—but God plans. How kind of Him to lead us in such pleasant paths.Praise His dear Name!

I must close else I weary you, but I love you very dearly.

Sincerely your own

Charlie

Hart, Mich.

Sat. P.M.

Postmark Aug. 16, 1913

My own Darling Charlie—

I received your dear letter last night after all the folks had gone home, and it is needless to say that I enjoyed it more than all the evening pleasure.

. . . My money is lasting beautifully. Yes, I think that it would be a good plan to get a catalogue from Young and Chaffee and perhaps from Winegars. Aren't they a furniture store? I got a letter from Edna, and they want us to stop at their house overnight on our way to Fenwick. What do you think about it? I suppose that would be Friday night (the day after the wedding).

Lester is tearing down the house this P.M. cutting a double doorway between the dining room and Ma's bedroom. Ma is sewing my carpet together. (It was woven in strips, which had to be sewn together by hand.) Marjorie is mending, Pearl is asleep, and Emma is writing to her Sweetheart. I surely think that she is the most fortunate girl in being engaged to the dearest preacher in the world.

Now I will tell you about the doings. In the first place I

had to get sick early yesterday morning, so that I was in great readiness to receive my company. But after taking a cup of hot ginger tea and scalding my feet in a bucket of water, I was able to sit up and do my share of talking. We girls tied the two quilts. Then we went out in the yard and the girls wrapped a quilt around me and made me a bridal veil of scarfs and put dahlias in my hair and a sunflower in my hand and a frame around me with one of Nellie Johnson's shoes on it and took my picture.

Then we gathered around the quilt and were taken together. Then the girls took the quilt and shook a cat in it, and the one that the cat ran out by, was the one who should next prepare quilts. The first was Rose, and the 2nd Hazel Cargill and the next Hazel Andrews. Then some of the girls wrote you a letter.Herman and Edna Graff tore it.Herman wanted to read it, but Edna wouldn't let him. Then he wanted to write and I said, "What have you got to say?"

He said, "I think that he is no better than I am." Ha, ha.

Someone spoke up and said, "Emma thinks that he is."

Herman traded tickets until he got Nellie Johnson's and mine for supper. Honestly, Dearest, I didn't mind their jollying a bit. I suppose that was because that I was so happy.

I do so love to receive your letters so often and so long. Talk about wearying me.You Darling, I don't weary of your talk except when you tell about being foolish and things like that, and yet I don't suppose that I would like you very well if you were continually praising yourself, as you never do.

Time flies, and still it drags.I dreamed the other night that we got married without any license and never thot about it until the next day, and then we got a license and had it done over again.

Beatrice McDonald had found out about the quilting bee, and she was telling Della that she thot the wedding was all off because when Roy (her brother) was up here (He was working for Shepherdsons for a time.) he was down cellar and heard us talking. (Ma had lost her husband in January, and her last son was married in June, so she protested about Emma marrying in September.) He didn't want to listen, and he didn't want to come up and us know that he had heard anything, so he sat there and did nothing.Ha,ha.

. . . I do not need to tell you who was most missed by me last night . . . I must send Pearl to the box with this letter, so I'll be looking for another letter soon. O,may our father bless His children in their efforts to please Him. I long for you, Sweetheart I want to be kissed. I want to hear your voice and see your face and feel your hand clasp mine, and I want to go along and help you a little.

From your own Emma

Chapter 27

Fenwick, Mich.
8/31/13
To my own Darling Emma,
It seems an age since I heard from my Sweetheart . . .

I promised Mr. Matice a long time ago that I would help him harvest beans—He wants me now for a while . . . so I'll stay and keep my word to him.But I wish you were here, and were to stay, Conference all over with. That doesn't hasten time a bit, however. But it is going rapidly—the four weeks you spoke of a short time ago is cut in two . . . Better have a merry time [?] while you can for Roy said, "You may be a long time tied." Ha.Pardon me, Emma, I don't mean it. Well, I hope we may be, for I anticipate happy times, tho perhaps extra burdens and cares for each of us yet we sincerely believe we can carry them together rather than be privileged to shake each other's hand once in six months. Oh, my Sweetheart, I long for you to help me with these people.I honestly don't believe I could get along without you much longer. Trust I won't have to, for Father continues to open the way—I see nothing, nor haven't since July that might hinder. So I surely feel to praise my heavenly Father's name tonight. Besides giving me the love of the dearest girl in the country, He gives me the love of Jesus continually. He is so precious to me. He has paid my fare clear thru into the City.

Only one more Sunday to shove the old wheel over the hills this year. (He rode his bicycle to serve Shanty Plains Church at Fenwick and the Orleans Church, seven miles away.). . . Fear I don't listen carefully enough to the Spirit's promptings and voice. I pray that He may repeat the opportunity (missed that morning).I'm full of mistakes. I greatly need help and leadership. Oh, that I might follow more closely my Father's leading! . . .

There are great furniture offers advertised now in the *PRESS*. But I love you, Sweetheart, and am becoming more and more anxious for the days to hasten. I look for a letter tomorrow.Goodnight.Sweet dreams.

Lovingly your own
Charlie

Hart, Mich.
8/29/13
My own Sweetheart—

I received your "sweet" letter tonight and I certainly enjoyed it as indeed I always do.

Monday 11:15 A.M. We are in the midst of moving, and I just finished cleaning the oil stove. (Lester had remodled the house to make two separate apartments, one for Ma and Pearl and other for him and Marjorie.) Last Thursday P.M. Mother and I went down to the store to buy a tablecloth and Aunt Lucy said that Della wanted to see me, so I went up to the house (Della Graff worked for Aunt Lucy.) and when I opened the sitting room door, I saw a roomful of girls. I said, "Della, Aunt Lucy said that you wanted to see me, so what will you have?"

So she took me by the arm and led me to the stair door and upstairs, and there was a mess of strings tied to a curtain pole and going in every direction around chair legs and under beds and everywhere, & I had to take hold of the end and follow it until I came to the other end. At the end of each was a present.Here is a list of them:

2 salad bowls—Bernice & Alberta (Eisenlohr), bed blanket—Aunt Nancy, table cloth, sample sack of flour & milk pitcher—Aunt Lucy, night dress—Uncle Marshall (Aunt Lucy had married an old beau, Marshall Randall. He had homesteaded in Kansas after being jilted and returned to Michigan after hearing of the death of Perl Thomas.), dresser scarf—Della, Dishpan—Edna Graff, frying pan—Gracie Baker, paring knife, spool of black thread, needle & 12 pants buttons—Vina Perry, guest towel—Erma Miller, guest towel—Irma Springmire, sofa pillow cover Beatrice, sofa pillow cover—Hazel Andrews, little basin—Margaret & Hazel, apron—Rose Perry, china plate—Altha Van Brocklin, china plate—Nellie Johnson, and Grandpa left a dollar at the store for me, and Lucille said that she had a little mustard dish for me. We had a nice supper at Della's too, and Della got it up. Don't you think that they are pretty good to us?

They said that they would soon have me pretty well broke in, but they didn't know about you.Ha.

Sat. Lester brought home a package and gave it to me.It contained a bedspread from Ma and an eight piece aluminum set . . . We'll soon have all we need, won't we, Honey?

I think that Edna only meant for us to stay Friday night on our way to Fenwick, and it isn't any out of the way is it? I wrote and told her we would come. (Edna Robbins was living at Sparta now with her mother, Rev. Ida Robbins, and her father.)

Jessie said that he would be in Fenwick on Monday if he could catch the morning train.

Ma is down to Vina's getting sweet corn to dry. Do you like it dried? . . .

3:30 P.M. I have just finished cutting a bushel of corn off from the cob, and I'm going down to see if your folks want me to help get supper for thrashers.

Lester and Marjorie are putting down their sitting room carpet . . .

I must go, but just think of 2 weeks from tonight. I feel awfully happy. Good bye my own Darling.

From Emma

(Written at the top of the letter)

I think the Conference address is Ashley.

Orleans

9/6/13

My own Darling Emma—

I came back down to these parts yesterday and found a most welcome letter from my Sweetheart also one from Herman. You may know which I read first . . . Don't believe we better buy any dishes 'till we reach our destination. Threshers are coming, so good bye for present. I love you dearly.

I am rounding up my studying a little.Guess I won't need to worry about that much more.It's noon—we did not quite get thru thrashing, but this is a strange crowd here, so while they are nooning, I'll write a few more lines to my intended bride.

Herman said he intended to go to M.A.C. (Michigan Agricultural College, later M.S.U.) said if I fainted and fell down, he would take my place. (Herman was to be the best man.) Ha.Poor lad. Disappointed.

Jake said . . . they would give us that sette setee [how spelled?] if we cared about having it. What do you think? . . . He is a dear good brother. The Lord bless those dear people of yours!

Well, this may be the last letter you receive from me for a time.I don't want to write you any more. <u>Good</u> reason why. Ha! Yes, I trust I won't have to write again for some long time. I may come home Saturday from Conference. I did not intend to tell you yet; but guess I better, for the mail is gone, so I can't send this 'till Monday. If you don't hear from me to the contrary you may look for me Sat. P.M. There will be so much to be done—packing, crating, etc. that I think I better come then. I will not have heard the appointments by that time, but I can figure to be in town Monday when J.E. comes and so hear our fate.I am getting a little anxious to know where they will send us, but I suppose we may get used to it (being placed by the Stationing Committee of the Annual Conference).

I guess by the sound of your letter we better get a couple piano boxes to pack the stuff in.The dear souls. Well, it is surely more than I expected. Did you receive the catalogs?

Well, I expect that two weeks from this P.M. we will both land in these parts as one. Ha. Then you won't have such a long name to write. No great loss without some small gain. Ha . . . The days cannot go too rapidly. Think we better go back to Grand Rapids from Sparta, thence to Orleans. Then we will arrive on the Plains at S.S. time and surprise them.

Stanton
Monday 9:00 A.M.
Postmark Sep 9, 1913
Hello Emma—

I left the letter I started for you Saturday down to Orleans in my suit case. Bro. Clawson is coming up to Bro. Baker's tonight and will bring it along. You will be looking for a letter all these days and look in vain.

I love you dearly this morning and trust this week will hasten past. I am now on my way to Greenville to buy some clothes . . . I will be able to report Conference claims full. Have $26.75 in my pocket and some more at Dulls. A little more came in at the last minute.

We organized a class in Orleans yesterday. Received two

on professon (not transfer). Praise God! Yesterday was a good day to my soul. I announced that I would endeavor to be with them again in two weeks—and then I don't expect to come alone. The time is almost gone—only a week after you receive this, and that won't seem so long for we will be a little nearer together than at present . . . 11:35 I am now waiting for dinner. They are fixing my suit. I found a nice serge at $13.75 at the big all wool store "The Man from Michigan."Got a $4.00 case and $3.50 shoes. I am afraid that at best I will make only a poor companion for <u>you</u>, but I am thankful that you are not inclined to look further . . . I love you most sincerely and am glad the time is so near at hand when you may become my very own wife. I need you and honestly believe the Lord may be able to use you to the salvation of souls and advancement of His cause. . . We will go to Conference in the morning. I haven't got my paper on Christian Endeavor interests quite ready as yet, but it won't take long to finish it.

. . . You dear girl, I can hardly wait 'till I can again clasp you in my arms.

J.E. failed to come last evening, but I received a card this morning saying he would give me the exam this P.M. at the Conference.

I am at Peabodys' in Sheridan waiting for the Grand Trunk train.

You will be looking all these days for a letter and none in evidence. Neglected Sweetheart. But I love you sincerely and will do the best I can to make up for it when I get home. But I must close.

With lots of love from your own Sweetheart.The one who loves you best –

Charlie

Chapter 28

North Michigan Annual Conference Ministers 1913

Emma met Charlie at the train Saturday evening with that slow horse. My, what a happy reunion it was! They met each other with outstretched arms, and walked hand in hand to the waiting buggy. Since the horse knew the way home, he was allowed to walk while Charlie held Emma in his arms and gave her the kisses she was waiting for. They did talk between kisses.

"Oh, before I forget to tell you, Emma, I passed my last exam, and I was granted an Annual Conference License, so now I am a member of the Annual Conference."

"Oh, Charlie, I'm so proud of you! When you became a Christian I didn't know you were going to be a preacher, but I'm very happy about it.I look forward to being able to help you."

"And another thing, George was not at Conference, but he wrote asking for a transfer to the Ontario Conference, so the Conference granted him the transfer."

"He wrote that they hoped to go to Canada.That seems so far away," she sighed."We'll almost never see them."

"I'm sure it'll be some time, but Canada's just on the other side of Port Huron. It's not as far as you think.Since I left before the Stationing Committee's Report, I can't tell you whether we'll be going back to Fenwick or somewhere else. Are you sure you're willing to go with me anywhere the Conference sends me?If you have any second thoughts, please tell me now."

"No, no, a thousand time no, I don't have second thoughts about marrying you and going wherever the Conference sends us," and she gladly accepted another kiss.

"I'll have to talk to Pa and Adelia about the things they have for us. He had a house full of things, and she had some of her own furniture and bedding that she brought, so they have extras that they'll share with us.Besides that, the Harry Harwoods left a bedroom suite at the parsonage in Fenwick that they said we're welcome to use as long as we're at Fenwick. If they ever move back from California, they'll need it. By that time we may be able to buy one of our own, Sweetheart."

"That'll be a wonderful help. Oh, Darling, it's been such fun making plans for our very own home."

"Yes, and they did roast you at the quilting party, didn't they?"

"Oh, yes.That was such fun. The poor cats, some descendents of Tiger Shep, a kitten I had when I was small, didn't know what was happening when we bounced them on the quilt."

"Did you bounce them all at once?"

"No, one at a time.We didn't hurt them.Just bounced them a little in the middle of the quilt. We bounced one, and he ran out by Rose. Then we found another and bounced it, and it ran out by . . ."

"Hazel Cargill and the next by Hazel Andrews."

She laughed, "You must have memorized my letter."

"I almost did," he laughed."Now no more letters.They were a wonderful help, but now I'm going to take you with me," he said and indulged in another kiss.

"I certainly hope so. I've been canning and sewing and preparing ever so many things to take, and those dear gifts from the shower—You should have seen the mess. I had to try to sort out all those strings and follow them to the gifts."

"That was very thoughtful of them, and it sounds like they made a game of it."

"They did.It was great fun, and I was <u>really</u> surprised!"

"Did I tell you Jake and Elsie are expecting a baby?"

"Yes, I take it the baby hasn't been born yet."

"No, they're still waiting.They're very happy about it."

"I'm sure they are. I'll be happy when we're expecting our first."

"Don't you think it would be better to wait for a few years?"

"Yes, I think we'll have our hands full for a while, learning to live with each other and doing the work the Father has for us. I agree that it would be better not to have children too soon, but I am looking forward to them."

"At the right time," he said as the horse took them into the Shepherdson driveway.

The next few days were filled with packing, crating in wooden packing cases to ship on the train, and oh, such happy preparations!

"Emma, Adelia wants you to go down and look at the bed and sewing machine she has for us," Charlie said as he greeted Emma with a loving kiss one evening.

"A sewing machine? Oh, Charlie, I'll be so happy to have my own sewing machine! I didn't know we'd have one so soon. Let's go right down and see it."

They took the buggy and drove to Hulls' house to look at the gifts being offered.

"Why, good evenin' Emma," Adelia greeted, taking Emma's hands. "You came to see the things, did you?"

"Yes, Charlie said you have a sewing machine for us."

"Oh, yes, I don't need two, so you can have his mother's. Here it is. It's a White. I'll be glad for you to have it. We're pretty crowded with my things and all his furniture and stuff."

"Thank you," Emma said, caressing the sewing machine, looking it over with an experienced eye. I'll be able to make very good use of this."

"Here's the bed you can have too," George Hull said, taking them into a bedroom. "And these pillows and sheets and quilts.Can you make use of all these things?"

"Oh, yes, thank you, Mr. and Mrs. Hull." It was hard for her to call the new wife Mrs. Hull, but she knew she should.

"We'll really appreciate them, Adelia," Charlie added.

The days passed so quickly.Charlie told Emma the next day, "I dismantled the bed and crated it, including some of the bedding in the box. I emptied the straw mattress. We'll find some fresh straw to fill it with when we get home."

"Home, yes, when we get home. This won't be home anymore, will it?"

"No, Darling," he said, taking her in his arms."We will have a new home, not really new, but it'll be our house for the time we live there," he said. "Aunty Dull and Uncle Jonas have been wonderful to me, but they will be glad for me to move down to the parsonage."

"And I'll have the pleasure of helping to make it into our very own home," she added, snuggling close for a kiss.

The wedding was to be on Thursday, September 18 at high noon, so they could catch the train for Grand Rapids. Emma added fine white cotton cloth to the bottom of her white eyelet graduation dress to make it longer for her wedding dress. She also made a shirred, white satin belt.Out of cardboard she cut a buckle for it and covered it with satin. Gracie Baker would be her bridesmaid and wear the pretty pink dress Emma had made for her.

Emma helped fry chicken on the morning of her wedding day. Her packing was all done. Everything was in readiness. Before noon the wedding party and families enjoyed a delicious chicken dinner at Shepherdsons' house, all except Emma. She was too excited to eat much.She packed a box lunch for her and Charlie to enjoy in the hotel room in Grand Rapids.

They went to the church in the two-seated buggy.Lena had decorated the church with lavender asters and made the bouquets for Emma and Gracie to carry. The bride carried pink geraniums, with cascading vines and a white ribbon bow. Gracie carried white geraniums with trailing vines and a pink bow.Emma's abundant long hair made a burnished blond bun like a crown on her head, with the sides waving softly, framing her face.

Charlie was handsome in his new black serge suit, supported by Herman Andrews.Charlie did not faint and fall, so the bride was his instead of Herman's.

Rev. J. E. Harwood performed the ceremony before the families and friends, including children who came across the corner from school to attend the wedding during their lunch hour.

Charlie, Emma, Grace, and Herman all signed the marriage certificate, said their farewells and before they knew it Rev. and Mrs. Charlie Hull were in the Shepherdson buggy with green fringe with Lester and Marjorie on their way to Hart to the train.

"Emma, I can't believe it. You're really my wife, my own darling wife. I like the sound of that word," Charlie said after waving goodbye to the loved ones in front of Sackrider Church.

"It's a dream come true. I'm so happy it hurts," Emma said, wiping the corner of her eye with a lace handkerchief, and placing her bouquet in the corner of the seat, so she could enjoy Charlie's embrace.

"Darling, I have a big surprise for you."

"A surprise?!What can it be?"

"Well, yesterday Pa gave me $85."

"$85?" she gasped.

Each of us boys is to have that amount when we turn 21 or get married, and since I'm getting married a couple months before I turn 21, Pa gave it to me yesterday. We inherited it from our mother. So just think how much fun we can have with that money tomorrow at Young and Chaffee's Furniture Store!"

"Oh, Charlie, that's wonderful! Do you think we can get a dining table and chairs with it?"

"Yes, and much more. I've been studying their ads, you know. I'm glad we got our cases of stuff shipped yesterday. They'll be waiting for us at the Fenwick Station."

Lester had not brought the slowest horses, and they arrived at the station with time to spare. They each carried some of the luggage to the waiting coach. (A spur of the railroad track went into Hart from the line between Muskegon and Pentwater, so the coach was there ready to be connected when the train arrived.)

Emma carried her bouquet, and Charlie helped her up the steps and into the coach, handing her a bag. Someone had been there ahead of them. The coach was beautifully decorated with pink and purple and white flowers, real flowers with pink and white ribbons. Emma caught her breath as she looked around, "Who did this?"she cried."It's so beautiful! I love it! Lester, who did this?"

"I'll never tell," he said with a twinkle in his eyes.

"Well, it's much nicer than old shoes," Charlie said, with a broad smile, as the train came steaming down the track.

Rev. Charlie and Emma Hull
(Taken in wedding clothes about a year after marriage)